He let out a ra
his arms arou
he leaned dow
**toward hers. Closer, closer. The tension
built between them until she thought
she might scream if he didn't kiss her
*right now.***

Bam!

He grabbed her and dove to the floor, his body
wrapped protectively around hers.

Bam! Bam!

She stared up at him in shock. "Were those
gunshots?"

"Rifle fire." He shook his head in disgust. "And I
don't have a gun because of the bail agreement."
He rose up, looking toward the front windows.

"Mason, my purse. You can use my gun." She
looked around, trying to remember where she'd left
it. There, on the floor by the end table.

He scrambled onto his knees and peered over
the back of the couch. "Hannah, stay here. Don't
move."

DEADLY DOUBLE-CROSS

LENA DIAZ

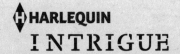

HARLEQUIN
INTRIGUE

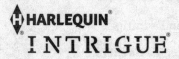

ISBN-13: 978-1-335-40179-3

Deadly Double-Cross

Copyright © 2021 by Lena Diaz

Recycling programs
for this product may
not exist in your area.

This edition published by arrangement with Harlequin Books S.A.

For questions and comments about the quality of this book,
please contact us at CustomerService@Harlequin.com.

Harlequin Enterprises ULC
22 Adelaide St. West, 40th Floor
Toronto, Ontario M5H 4E3, Canada
www.Harlequin.com

Printed in U.S.A.

Lena Diaz was born in Kentucky and has also lived in California, Louisiana and Florida, where she now resides with her husband and two children. Before becoming a romantic suspense author, she was a computer programmer. A Romance Writers of America Golden Heart® Award finalist, she has also won the prestigious Daphne du Maurier Award for Excellence in Mystery/Suspense. To get the latest news about Lena, please visit her website, lenadiaz.com.

Books by Lena Diaz

Harlequin Intrigue

The Justice Seekers

Cowboy Under Fire
Agent Under Siege
Killer Conspiracy
Deadly Double-Cross

The Mighty McKenzies

Smoky Mountains Ranger
Smokies Special Agent
Conflicting Evidence
Undercover Rebel

Tennessee SWAT

Mountain Witness
Secret Stalker
Stranded with the Detective
SWAT Standoff

CAST OF CHARACTERS

Mason Ford—The former chief of police, and founder of The Justice Seekers, made his hometown pay dearly for the corruption that led to the murder of his oldest brother. But now someone wants revenge, and they're willing to frame him as a killer to get it.

Hannah Cantrell—This crime scene data analyst must choose between her family and Mason, the man she's falling in love with.

Hank Abrams—This deputy could be an innocent pawn in the killer's plan to frame Mason. Or he could be the killer.

Gary Donnelly—Hank's friend and coworker, he may be the mastermind behind everything going wrong in Beauchamp, Louisiana.

Paul Murphy—A captain in the police department where Mason was once chief, is he part of the old guard that covered up the murder of Mason's brother?

Warren Knoll—District attorney of Sabine Parish, Louisiana. Mason's life hangs on the line when Knoll inserts himself into the investigation of the alleged frame-up.

Eli Dupree—This newest member of The Justice Seekers isn't fitting in with the team. Mason hates that he suspects his fellow Louisianan of being involved in the conspiracy.

Wyatt Ford—Mason's youngest brother, Wyatt blames Mason for their oldest brother's death. Is it because he believes Mason is responsible? Or is Wyatt trying to cover his own sins?

Olivia Ford—Mason's little sister has never recovered from their brother's death. Is it because she feels guilty?

Chapter One

Mason Ford vowed to pay more attention next year when his assistant chose the date for the company's fall hayride, because it was incredibly difficult acting the benevolent boss on the anniversary of his brother's unsolved murder.

Then again, maybe having the hayride this morning was a good thing. A new, happy memory to help dull a horrific one.

He'd forgotten the charm and beauty of the eight-mile arts and crafts loop just east of Gatlinburg, Tennessee. And it certainly wasn't a hardship admiring the colorful fall leaves as a pair of enormous draft horses pulled the eighteen-foot wagon through the Smoky Mountains. It was the exact opposite of his Louisiana hometown's evergreens, swamps and bayous without a mountain in sight.

Moving here, escaping the daily reminders of his old life, was the only thing that had kept him sane through the years. Well, that, and being able to hire others like him, men and women whose law enforcement careers had been destroyed through no fault of their own. Being a Justice Seeker gave all of them a chance at redemption and an opportunity to continue their true calling—helping others.

The modern-day Camelot he'd created investigated crimes and protected others, with one important distinction from their law enforcement counterparts. The twelve Seekers who worked for him, his Knights of the Round Table, would bend or break the law if necessary to keep someone safe. It was infinitely preferable to prevent a murder than to hunt down an offender *after* they'd violated a useless restraining order and killed someone. The Seekers sometimes played fast and loose with the law. But Mason's team helped their allies in law enforcement so much that they were usually willing to turn a blind eye.

The enormous success of his company was bittersweet since it owed its existence to his older brother's death. Mason had been the chief of police in his hometown of Beauchamp, Louisiana, when Landon was framed and convicted with blinding speed, then killed in prison while Mason was scrambling to exonerate him. It was his subsequent civil suit against the corrupt town leaders who'd been instrumental in his brother's sham of a conviction that had given him the millions to start his company. But he'd give up all his wealth, without hesitation, if it would bring Landon back.

Since that wasn't possible, he'd done the only thing he could to honor his memory. He'd secretly continued the investigation on his own, trying to figure out the identity of that one last person behind the conspiracy that had resulted in his brother's conviction and murder. But justice was proving to be frustratingly elusive. Which was why he'd soon head home for his annual appointment with a bottle of Jack Daniel's to grieve for his brother in private and curse his own failure to solve the riddle of Landon's death.

A burst of laughter sounded from the far end of the wagon. Former FBI profiler, Bryson Anton, was laughing at something his fiancée, Teagan, had said. Beside them, former secret service agent, Gage Bishop—Mason's closest friend and the very first Seeker he'd ever hired—grinned at his girlfriend, Harper. It was truly amazing to see Bishop looking so happy these days. Harper was exactly what the normally morose Bishop needed, a balm to his battered soul. It was a balm to Mason's as well, seeing how much his team seemed to be enjoying the outing.

Except, perhaps, the newest member of The Justice Seekers.

Eli Dupree sat by himself a couple of hay bales away from Mason, splitting his time between watching the scenery and surreptitiously glancing at the other Seekers. He was relatively new to Gatlinburg, having arrived only a few months ago. A former police officer and Louisianan, like Mason, Eli had been the victim of a crooked conspiracy in Baton Rouge. But unlike Mason, he hadn't been able to turn his misfortune into something good and had struggled to make ends meet.

Mason considered himself fortunate that Eli had looked him up and asked for a job. The timing was perfect, since Mason had been searching for a suitable replacement for their fallen Seeker, Seth Knox. And

Mason was thrilled to help someone from his home state. He just hoped Eli would learn to appreciate Tennessee the way Mason did, and that he'd eventually fit in with the rest of the team.

When the wagon slowed and made the final turn off Highway 321 into the Family Dollar store's parking lot, where they'd all parked their personal vehicles earlier, Eli motioned toward Mason's black BMW. "Looks like someone's waiting for you."

A familiar red convertible was parked in the spot beside his with an even more familiar-looking platinum blonde standing between the two cars. Mason let out a deep sigh. Why had she chosen today, of all days, to show up again? It had been a couple of years since the last time she'd made the long trip here in her ongoing campaign to win him back. Plus, he'd heard she'd gotten engaged again. Apparently it had been too optimistic on his part to assume that would mean she'd finally stop what could only be called harassment.

A shadow fell across him. He looked up to see Bishop in full former secret service agent mode, dark sunglasses in place, pistol bulging beneath his light jacket, a deadly serious look on his face. "I can take care of this. Just say the word."

Dalton Lynch, a former policeman from Montana, stepped beside him, straightening the black Stetson he was never without. "Need me to block Guinevere's car while you make your getaway?"

Bishop gave Dalton a warning look over the top of his shades. "I've got this, cowboy."

Dalton bumped his shoulder against Bishop.

Bishop held his ground and returned the gesture, his frown growing fierce.

Dalton grinned, not at all intimidated.

A few feet away, Eli glanced back and forth between them. "Guinevere?"

Mason narrowed his eyes at Dalton, before answering. "Her *name* is Audrey Broussard. Years ago, *many* years ago, we were engaged."

"Lancelot must have frozen her credit cards," Dalton said. "No offense to your charms, boss, but I can give you several million reasons why she wants to be on your arm again."

Eli's look of curiosity turned to confusion. "Lancelot? Wait, didn't he sleep with Guinevere behind King Arthur's back?"

Dalton had the grace to wince before his expression sobered. "Let Bishop and me take care of this, boss. You don't even have to talk to her."

Mason's throat tightened when he realized the rest of his team had silently moved to stand behind Dalton and Bishop, letting him know they were there to support him, as well. Except for Bishop, none of the Seekers knew the details about what had happened in his hometown years ago. But all of them were making it clear whose side they were on.

He had to clear his throat, twice, before trusting his voice enough to speak. "I couldn't ask for a better team. You're always there for me and each other. But this… this is something I have to take care of myself."

They stepped back so he could make his way down the center aisle through the hay bales and dismount from the wagon. But before heading to his impatient-looking former fiancée, he turned around to address his employees. No, his *family*. His *chosen* family, rather than the one he was born into. He cherished every single one of them.

"I hope you all had a great time. Enjoy the Fall Festival in town today and Sunday. As a bonus, take Monday off, with pay. The last thing I need is a bunch of hungover gun-toting yahoos dragging into the office after partying hard all weekend."

Their cheers gave him the strength he needed to face whatever Audrey was about to dish out. When he reached his car, he nodded in greeting and leaned against his driver's door. "Audrey."

She mimicked his pose, leaning against the passenger side of her sports car. "Mason. Still wearing business suits everywhere, I see. Even on a hayride." Her red lips curved in a practiced smile.

"Image is everything." He returned her smile, taking in her stilettos and silky black dress that couldn't come close to keeping her warm. The early morning temp this time of year, this high up in the mountains, was probably hovering around fifty degrees, if that. He'd offer her his suit jacket, but he could see a fur coat draped over the passenger seat through the window behind her. She'd obviously chosen to go for looks, instead of warmth. And she did look good, always had. Even in grade school she'd been the prettiest girl on the playground.

"You're as beautiful as ever." On closer inspection, though, there were dark circles under her eyes that her makeup failed to completely conceal. And she seemed tired, pale. Even her hair seemed to lack the luster it usually had. Since he'd never seen her looking anything less than perfect, he couldn't help wondering if something was wrong. "Is everything all right? Do you feel okay?"

Her cornflower blue eyes widened and she self-consciously patted her hair. "I'm fine. Why do you ask?"

She was probably just tired after the twelve-plus-hour drive from Beauchamp to Gatlinburg. Maybe she'd driven through the night to get here and hadn't stopped at a hotel yet to rest. "No reason. Just small talk." He shifted against the car and crossed his arms. "I heard you and Thibodeaux got engaged. Congratulations."

"If that's what your baby sister told you in those gossip sessions over the phone, then she's either out of touch with the local grapevine or just being mean. Richard and I broke up a few months ago." She tilted her chin defiantly.

"Olivia doesn't have a mean bone in her body. But it's been a while since our last phone call, so I didn't realize your status had changed. I'm sorry that things didn't work out between you and Richard."

And he was. Even though Audrey had destroyed the friendship between Mason and Richard Thibodeaux, Mason sympathized with her over losing him. It had taken her years to get him to give her a ring. With him gone, there weren't many more prospects left in the small town of Beauchamp, since her main preferred qualification in a relationship was money, or at least the prospect of decent future earnings.

She shrugged, pretending it didn't matter. "He moved to Texas. The man I left you for has now left me. That probably makes you happy, doesn't it? Poetic justice?"

"No, it doesn't. You deserve to find that special someone just as much as anyone else. I assumed that person was Richard. I'm sorry that it wasn't."

She stared at him a long moment, before blinking back the suspicious moisture in her eyes. "He was always my second choice."

"Audrey, don't."

"I mean it, Mason. You and I were good together. Really good. Give me another chance. Give *us* another chance. Forgive my one little mistake."

"Sleeping with my best friend, then throwing your engagement ring in my face in the middle of the town square isn't what I call one little mistake."

"It was only the one time. I turned to Richard for comfort. I was upset at you for filing that silly lawsuit. You sued half my friends. No one would talk to me anymore."

"I may have been a lovesick fool back then, but I wasn't blind. We both know it was more than once, with more than one guy."

Her face turned a bright pink.

"As to the *silly* lawsuit," he continued, "it was the only way I could obtain any kind of justice for Landon's death. Those so-called friends of yours helped conceal and falsify evidence. If it wasn't for them, my brother wouldn't have been convicted, sent to prison and slaughtered before I could prove his innocence. The infidelity

I could forgive. You supporting the people responsible for my brother's murder? That, I can never forgive."

Her eyes flashed with anger. "It's so easy for you to judge me. Saint Mason can do no wrong, always better than anyone else. Maybe someone should judge you for a change, make you pay for what you've done to others."

Her lightning-quick mood swing surprised him, but no more than what she'd said. Other than bringing criminals to justice, he'd always tried to treat others with respect, especially Audrey. No matter what had happened between them, he'd loved her once, had planned to spend the rest of his life with her. Part of him would always care about her. "I'm not sure what you're talking about. What do you think I've done?"

She opened her mouth as if to say something, then seemed to think better of it. When she regained control, she drew a steadying breath. "Obviously, coming here was a mistake. I shouldn't have wasted my time thinking you'd soften toward me. You probably never loved me in the first place."

He'd loved her *too* much. That was his downfall. His mind had known the relationship was doomed long before his heart would accept the painful truth.

"Why are you really here? Especially today."

She arched a brow. "What's special about today?"

Her tone told him what she refused to admit. She knew the significance of the date and must have chosen it hoping he'd be more vulnerable, maybe more amenable to whatever it was that she wanted. "Did you come here for money? Have you burned through what I gave you after I won the civil suit?"

Her face pinkened again. "It's been seven years since the lawsuit. If I had spent it all in that long a time, I'd hardly qualify it as *burning* through the money."

Since he'd given her close to a million dollars, he wasn't sure that he agreed. "How much do you need?"

She stared at him incredulously. "Are you seriously offering to pay me off?"

"It's not a payoff. It's an offer to help. If you're in financial trouble, I'm happy to give you some money. As a friend, nothing more. But after this, I'm done. It's not fair to either of us for you to keep coming up here. You should go home and never come back."

"Never come back." She gave him a tight smile. "Careful what you wish for."

He frowned. "What's going on in Beauchamp? Is someone bothering you? Do you need help?"

She clutched her keys in her hand and rounded her car to the driver's side. "If you think I'm here to hire The Justice Seekers, you've lost your mind. Your little company's a joke back home."

"A joke, huh?"

She gave him a mutinous glare.

He considered telling her his *little* company grossed over ten million dollars, in a bad year, and that his investments generated far more than that. It was true that half of his clients either paid little or no money, because they couldn't afford his usual fees. The Seekers never turned someone away based on finances if they had a legitimate, urgent need and Mason felt his company could help them. But the rest of their clients more than made up for that financial gap.

Wealthy businessmen were willing to pay a small fortune to protect their assets or to quietly resolve problems involving their families. Not to mention the lucrative hostage rescues the Seekers performed for corporations who didn't want the public to know their CEOs had been taken captive on a trip out of the country. They couldn't risk having their stock tank on that news. Business for the Seekers was good. More than good. But telling her that would only sound like bragging.

It didn't matter anyway. His hometown was no fan of him, no matter what he accomplished in life. The feeling was mutual. The secret trips he made to Beauchamp twice a year under the guise of vacations were just that—secret. Even his own family didn't know he was there, since none of them were willing to risk being seen with him any more than Audrey was, once he'd filed that lawsuit.

No one in Beauchamp ever saw past his alias and the movie-set-worthy disguise he'd paid a small fortune to obtain. Which was exactly what he wanted. He wasn't there for socializing. He went there to work on his brother's case, not that he'd made any real progress. It was taking far too long to get the locals to trust a supposed businessman on vacation twice a year and open up about anything they'd seen or knew. One of these days he'd have to put his life on hold and spend a couple of months in Beauchamp to really dig into the case. Maybe then he'd finally get justice for Landon.

"If you're not here for money, then why are you here?

We both know you're not really pining for me. Not after all this time. What's going on?"

Again, she looked like she wanted to say something important, but she just shook her head. Without another word, she got into her car.

Mason had to jump back to avoid having his feet run over by her tires. He watched her tear out of the parking lot, going dangerously fast around a curve in the mountain road before disappearing from sight.

He stood there a long time, reflecting on their oddly short and bizarre conversation. But no matter how hard he tried, he couldn't make sense of it. Her past visits had been far less confrontational. They'd usually go to dinner, take a walk in the mountains, talk about old times—the good ones, before everything went bad. But no matter what he said or did, these trips of hers always ended the same way—with her storming off. If he lived to be a hundred, he didn't think he'd ever understand her. Which was a sad statement, considering they'd known each other for several decades.

Half an hour later he was standing at his kitchen sink, holding a shot glass of whiskey. Before taking a sip, he made the same toast he'd made on every anniversary of his brother's death. "Landon, I promise I'll never stop trying to find out who really killed Mandy DuBois. I vow to get justice for you, and for our family. Rest in peace, big brother." He tossed the shot down, grimacing at the burn. But he knew from experience the next one would go down easier, and the next after that. The more drunk he got, the better the whiskey tasted.

He was reaching for the bottle to take it to the family

room when a floorboard creaked behind him. He jerked to the side, grabbing his gun from its holster. A masked man dived at him, tackling him to the ground. Mason arched off the floor, bucking the man off even as other masked intruders swarmed into the room. He swung his pistol around and squeezed the trigger.

Pop, pop, pop.

One of the men dropped to the floor, groaning.

"Suck it up, Hank," another man yelled. "You've got a vest on, you wuss."

Mason lunged to his feet.

Someone slammed into his back, knocking him to the floor again. There were five of them, all wearing masks.

"Grab his arms, Gary. Good grief. He's just one man. Guys, help him."

Mason rolled and swung his gun around, but the one named Gary crashed down on his arm, knocking the gun away.

The rest threw themselves on his legs, his other arm, his ribs.

Mason bucked and thrashed, desperately trying to throw them off.

"Sit on his back, sit on his back! Hank, quit rolling around on the floor. Get the syringe. Hurry!"

One of the men slammed Mason's jaw against the floor. A coppery taste filled his mouth.

"Do it!" one of them yelled again. "Hurry up."

A sharp pain pierced the side of Mason's neck. He tried to jerk his head back but the weight of all the bodies on him was too much. A heaviness flooded his limbs. They'd drugged him. He tried to twist away but he couldn't seem to make his body obey his commands. He slumped against the floor, his muscles twitching, useless. His lungs seized as he gasped for breath, trying to draw in much-needed oxygen. Spots swam in front of his eyes.

"Good gravy, how much did you give him? We don't want to kill him. She wants him alive."

She? Were they talking about Audrey? Had the conversation in the parking lot been a test that he'd failed, and she'd sent these thugs to teach him some sort of lesson? He'd never known her to be violent in the past. Maybe this was related to his company, revenge because the Seekers had helped the police put someone's family member in prison.

He struggled to keep his eyes open, to fight back. But his strength melted away like ice on a hot road in summer. His eyelids fluttered closed and he surrendered to the darkness.

Chapter Two

Somewhere along the way, Mason had heard that there were over seven trillion nerves in the human body. As he blinked his bleary eyes at the ceiling above his bed, he was certain he could feel every one of them. Everything ached.

He blinked again, the bright sunlight pouring through the nearby window making it hard to focus. Wait. Bright sunlight? Normally he was up before dawn. Why was he lying in bed so late?

Maybe because his entire body was throbbing with pain?

If he'd wrestled with a baby elephant and it had jumped up and down on his back a few times, he couldn't imagine he'd feel more battered and bruised than he did right now. Maybe he'd wrestled *two* baby elephants.

He drew a deep breath and immediately regretted it. The pain nearly made him pass out. What had he done? Drunk the entire bottle of Jack Daniel's and a couple bottles of vodka as chasers? No. He'd only had one drink, hadn't he? He'd been standing at the kitchen window, tossing down a shot. Then he'd reached for the bottle and—

Someone had broken into his house.

No, that was wrong. They'd already been there when he got home. They were lying in wait. When he'd had his back turned in the kitchen, they'd attacked. At least five men. Gary, Hank and others whose names he hadn't heard. They'd tackled him to the floor and the one named Hank had jammed a needle into his neck.

He gingerly felt along the back of his neck. Sure enough, it was sore. The way it would feel if a clumsy idiot not used to giving shots had stabbed him with a needle. He was lucky to be alive. Or was he? They would have killed him if that was their goal. He certainly couldn't have stopped them. God knows he'd tried his best. So why drug him, beat him to a pulp, then leave? It didn't make any sense.

He stared at the ceiling overhead, then frowned. The patterns were all wrong, too elegant, too…complicated. The ceiling should have been simple, not ornate. And white, not this creamy yellow color reminiscent of watered-down lemonade.

This wasn't his house.

He jerked upright, then groaned as pain lanced through his body. Taking slow, shallow breaths, he fought through it and looked around. Instead of wooden blinds on the window by the bed, long golden curtains fluttered in the cool breeze. Music wafted through the opening, faint and hauntingly familiar. The kind he'd grown up with, had danced to, had sung out of tune to along with his drunk fraternity brothers in far too many bars on way too many nights. Jazz.

Familiar smells filtered in through the open window too. Hot asphalt. Garbage. Honeysuckle. And… beignets?

A sense of impending doom shot through him as he forced his aching body to his feet and crossed stiffly to the window. A black wrought iron railing ran along the balcony outside. He was in the second floor bedroom of someone else's home. Whose, he didn't know. But there was no doubt *where*, as he looked down into a narrow alley with garbage cans set out for collection, then across that same alley at the backs of other homes.

They were all brightly painted, with elaborate decorative molding and fancy wrought iron balconies, many adorned with cheap, colorful beads—the kind they tossed at Mardi Gras. As impossible as it seemed, he was in Louisiana. And if his memory was correct, this particular street was in historic downtown Beauchamp in Sabine Parish, not far from where Landon and his girlfriend used to live.

He swore and automatically reached for his pistol on the nightstand by the bed, both surprised and dismayed to find it there. Whatever was going on couldn't be good. Of that he was certain. He had to get out of here, fast, before whoever had brought him here came back.

Thankfully, there was no need to search for his clothes. He was still wearing the dove gray suit he'd worn at the hayride, although it was considerably more wrinkled now.

Cursing his aches and pains, he ran across the room

and threw open the bedroom door. He was at the end of a long hallway but could see light coming from his left, probably the stairs. He bolted for them, taking two at a time. At the bottom, he started toward the front door, then froze.

A woman's body lay a few feet from the base of the stairs, in a pool of blood. The top of her scalp was gone, but there was enough hair remaining to show it was blond. Platinum blond. Or it had been, when she'd been in Gatlinburg.

"Audrey, good Lord, no." His voice broke as he stared down at her still perfect-looking face, turned toward him. Her eyes were cloudy and unseeing, no longer that cornflower blue so unique to her. There was no point in checking for a pulse. She was gone. The damage too severe.

What in the world had happened? Who would want to hurt her like this? He swore again and bowed his head, then sucked in a sharp breath when he saw the gun in his hand. The jagged, confusing images swirling through his mind suddenly crystallized into a coherent, terrifying reality.

Someone had drugged him.

They'd gone to incredible lengths to kidnap him and bring him back to the town he both loved and hated, a place crawling with enemies who wanted him dead.

They'd left him here, with a gun, with the dead body of his former lover, the same woman who'd confronted him in front of over a dozen witnesses in Gatlinburg on the anniversary of his brother's murder.

Ah hell.

Someone was setting him up. And the bastards had killed Audrey to do it. If he didn't get out of here, right now, he was royally screwed. He whirled toward the front door.

It flew open, slamming back against the wall.

"Police, freeze, don't move!" At least a dozen uniformed police officers surged through the opening into the house.

"Drop your weapon! Drop your weapon!"

He dropped the pistol and slowly raised his hands. "Officers, this isn't what it looks like. I didn't kill her. I don't even know how I got—"

Two of the police barreled into him, tackling him to the ground.

His aching ribs protested the abuse but he forced himself to go limp. Whoever was responsible for this insanity likely expected him to resist, giving the police an excuse to shoot him. This was a fight for his life, but not a physical one. He'd have to use all his wits to survive.

They rolled him onto his belly, jerked his hands behind his back and fastened handcuffs on his wrists with a painful click.

One of the officers patted him down while another barked orders. Still more fanned out, no doubt looking for accomplices. They needn't have bothered. Mason knew this story. He'd read it before. Except that time, it had been his older brother, Landon, who'd been found standing over a body. And it was his brother's girlfriend, Mandy DuBois, lying dead on the floor.

"Hank, Gary, get him up," the lead policeman yelled.

Hank? Gary? Mason jerked against their hold, but it was too late. They hauled him to his feet.

The leader stepped in front of Mason. "I'm Captain Paul Murphy. Remember the name. Because I'm the one who's going to see that you go to prison for murder, you slimy piece of scum. With any luck, maybe Louisiana will start carrying out the death penalty again, just for you." He motioned at Hank and Gary. "Get him out of here."

Chapter Three

Mason gritted his teeth as he was shoved out of the elevator onto the second floor of the police station by the two officers he now knew were Hank Abrams and Gary Donnelly. The one named Donnelly yanked his arm, hard. Mason pretended to lose his balance and fell against him, slamming the man's hip into a nearby desk, equally hard.

"My bad." Mason smiled.

Donnelly cursed and shoved away from the desk. "You did that on purpose," he accused, as Abrams tugged Mason's other arm.

Mason held his ground, ignoring Abrams. "You and I both know that you and your little friend here were in my home in Gatlinburg. Drugging me and setting me up for Audrey's murder. You may have the upper hand right this minute. But that won't last. By the time I'm done, you'll both either be in prison or dead."

"Is that a threat, Ford?"

"It's a promise, Donnelly. And if you yank my arm one more time, I'm going to break your damn nose."

Donnelly's face turned red. "I dare you to try."

"Take one step closer and I'll take that dare."

He hesitated, looking unsure.

"Cluck, cluck." Mason purposely incited him.

Sure enough, Donnelly lunged forward. Mason jammed his elbow against the other man's face with a sickening crunch. He yelled and grabbed his nose, which was already dripping blood. Donnelly glared his rage, then charged Mason again. Abrams intervened, letting Mason go to grab Donnelly in a bear hug. He harshly whispered for him to knock it off and stop making a scene.

Mason took full advantage of the chaos as a couple of other officers in the near-empty squad room headed toward Donnelly. Backing against another desk, Mason feigned a look of boredom as he grabbed a pair of sunglasses he'd spotted moments earlier and clutched them between his cuffed hands.

While Abrams tried to settle Donnelly down, Mason snapped one of the arms off the glasses, then snapped it in half again to give himself a thin, clean edge. He slid his makeshift shim into the ratcheting mechanism of one of his cuffs, jamming it in as hard as he could while trying not to grimace at the pain when the cuffs ratcheted tighter.

"Hey, hey, what's going on over there?" a detective from the other side of the room called out.

Abrams shoved his partner back, giving him a warning glance as they both straightened. "Just a minor disagreement. We're cool." He waved away the other officers who'd come over to help, then glanced at Mason, as if just remembering he was there.

Mason did his best to keep his arms and shoulders steady so he didn't give any indication that his hands were furiously busy behind his back. He shoved the shim again, between the metal teeth and the ratchet. The cuff ratcheted one more slot, then another, then disengaged. The metal arm of the cuff opened and slid off his right wrist. He grabbed it between his fingers just in time to keep it from clinking against the other cuff, while keeping his hands linked together. To anyone looking at him, he was still handcuffed.

Abrams argued with the detective who'd crossed the room to check on them while Donnelly pressed some tissues to his nose.

Mason glanced behind him to the corner of the room where his office used to be. Sure enough, gold letters on the solid, steel security door still said Chief of Police. Hopefully the inside of the office hadn't changed either, or his hastily concocted plan was going to end almost as soon as it began.

He didn't know who was behind his kidnapping, or Audrey's murder, but his experiences long ago told him one thing for sure. If they got him into a holding cell, he'd never come out alive. There were too many crooks still running this town, in spite of everything he'd done to try to clean it up. And the mysterious "she" the masked men at his home had mentioned was still calling the shots for the police she'd bought and paid for.

"Come on, Gary," Hank gritted out. "Cool your heels. Let's just get him to booking."

"Chief Ford? Is that you?" Another detective crossed the room, a big burly man Mason recognized as one of his former deputies, Harvey Latimer. Back then, everyone had called him Al because of his resemblance to the Twinkie-eating policeman in the movie *Die Hard*. When someone found a collection of Twinkies in his desk, it had sealed the nickname.

"Al?" Mason asked.

He grinned. "You remember. What are you doing here?" He stopped in front of Mason, his grin fading. "And what the hell are you doing in handcuffs? Donnelly, Abrams, have you lost your minds? This is one of our former police chiefs. He's the one who cleaned up this place, got rid of the riffraff around here." He gave them both a contemptuous look. "Not that it stopped more from coming after he left."

"Mind your own business," Abrams muttered. "He killed someone. Was caught red-handed."

"What he meant to say," Mason corrected, "was that these two jokers and a handful of others broke into my home in Tennessee, beat the hell out of me and drugged me. I woke up here, in a house I've never been in before, with the police crashing in the door. Once again, someone in my family is being framed for murder. Only this time, it's me. Amazing how this stuff always happens in Sabine Parish, don't you think?"

Al's frown became incredulous as he turned toward his fellow officers. "What's going on, Abrams? Donnelly? You know anything about him being attacked and kidnapped?"

Donnelly rolled his eyes and grabbed another handful of tissues from a nearby desk. "What a crock." His voice was muffled. He rolled his eyes again and threw the tissues down. "It's halfway across the country from here to Gatlinburg. If someone broke in his house yesterday, he wouldn't be here in Beauchamp today. Do the math. It don't add up."

Mason arched a brow. "I don't remember mentioning Gatlinburg, or the timing."

Donnelly's face reddened.

"It's a twelve-hour drive," Mason continued. "More than enough time for me to be here now. *Do the math.* Or didn't you pass basic math in elementary school?"

He took a menacing step toward Mason.

Al shoved him and moved between them, his back to Mason. "That's enough. Looks to me like we need to get the chief to figure out what's going on—"

Mason yanked Al's gun out of his holster, then slung his left arm around Abrams's throat, jerking him backward. Using him as a shield, his gun aimed at Abrams's temple, he backed toward the corner office.

Al put his hands on his hips. "Now, Chief Ford, why'd you have to go and do a thing like that? I was on your side."

"Sorry, Al. But this is life or death. Mine. And I'm not putting my fate in the hands of two of the men responsible for kidnapping me and setting me up. As far as I know, one of them murdered Audrey Broussard too. At the very least, they know who did." He jerked Abrams, making the man grunt in pain. It was surprisingly satisfying.

The handful of officers at other desks pointed their guns at Mason, who was almost to the office now.

"Hey, hey," Abrams choked out. "You're pointing those at me too."

The officers glanced uncertainly at each other, then slowly lowered their weapons.

Mason's back bumped against the door, stopping him. "Al, is Holloway still the chief?"

"Nah. He was over his head from day one and was bound and determined to take this place down with him. We've had a string of chiefs since then. No one sticks around very long. Our new mayor brought in Mitch Landry a couple of years ago, from nearby Many, hoping he could finally finish cleaning out the cockroaches around here after the good cleaning you gave the place." He eyed Donnelly. "But those nasty things are hard to get rid of."

Donnelly glared at him as if he wanted to shoot him.

"Is he in his office?" Mason asked. "I need to talk to him, make sure he knows what's really going on."

"He's out of town at a convention, in New Orleans, over four hours away."

Donnelly frowned. "I thought—"

"Well that would be a first, wouldn't it?" Al gritted out. "Shut up. And wipe your dang nose before you drip blood on the carpet."

Donnelly blasted him with a string of obscenities as he wiped his nose, leaving a red smear across his face.

"I'm happy to wait until the chief's available." Mason turned the knob behind him and pushed the door open. He gave Abrams a huge shove and jumped inside, then slammed the door. After locking it, he tucked his gun in his waistband and grasped a filing cabinet to the left of the door. It was full, far too heavy to scoot across the low-pile carpet. Instead, he heaved and strained, toppling it over like a tree. It fell sideways with a deafening bang, the drawers hanging half open and folders spilling onto the floor. He'd pretty much destroyed the cabinet. But it did the job, blocking the door from opening.

"Well, this is awkward."

He whirled around at the sound of the feminine voice behind him. When he saw the young woman sitting behind the desk by the window about fifteen feet away, he swore.

Her brows arched and she tucked her wavy, long brown hair behind her ears. "Not the reaction I'd normally hope for from a gorgeous man like yourself. Then again, the handcuffs dangling from your left wrist are a relationship nonstarter for me. I'm Hannah Cantrell. And you are?"

"Really sorry that I didn't realize you were here before I blocked the door." A muffled banging noise sounded behind him, rattling the door on its frame.

"That makes two of us. But since they're ramming the door, I'm guessing you aren't going to move the filing cabinet to let me out."

"That wouldn't be my first choice." The banging sounded again. "Excuse me a moment. I need to take care of this." He drew his gun, keeping it pointed away from her.

"You're not going to shoot anyone, are you?" she asked.

"Not on purpose."

She motioned toward the door. "Then by all means. Carry on. I'll wait."

He gave her a puzzled look, but nodded. Half turning, keeping her in his peripheral vision, he yelled, hoping Al could hear him. "Get away from the door or I'll shoot."

The loud bang sounded again. The door held fast as designed when he'd beefed up the physical security during his tenure as chief. But the frame around it shuddered. He looked back and spoke in a low voice. "Hannah? They haven't built a third story on this place since the last time I was here, have they? I didn't see the outside of the building when they drove me into the parking garage."

"Not that I've noticed. And I work here every weekday, so I'm pretty sure it's just two stories."

"Thank you."

"You're welcome."

"You might want to cover your ears."

She obligingly put her hands over both ears. He pointed his pistol toward the ceiling and squeezed the trigger.

The gunshot was incredibly loud in the confined space. His own ears were ringing. But at least the siege on the door had stopped. "The next time someone tries to knock the door down, I'll shoot right through it," he yelled.

A moment later, Al's voice called out, sounding muffled. "We'll stop trying to get in. Just don't shoot, all right?"

"Did you call the police chief?"

"What?" Al's voice was barely audible.

Mason cleared his throat, regretting that he'd put such a solid, thick door on the office as he yelled his question again.

Al answered, "He's on his way. But like I said, he's a good four hours out, only a little less with lights and sirens. Traffic and road conditions and all that."

"Just let me know when he gets here." He shoved the pistol in the back of his waistband and headed to the desk. "Hannah, thank you for your cooperation. I have no intention of hurting you."

"Good to know. Who are you?"

"Oh. Sorry. Mason Ford."

Her eyes widened, and he realized they were an incredible shade of green.

"*The* Mason Ford? The former police chief who brought this town to its knees with an FBI corruption investigation eight years ago? And sued it, successfully, for millions of dollars in a wrongful death suit? *That* Mason Ford?"

He winced. "One and the same. Trust me. Coming here today in such a public fashion was never my intention. My visits normally stay below the radar."

"Visits? Then you've been back here since you left? I mean, since your, well, rather ignominious departure?"

He hesitated, realizing he'd already said more than he'd intended.

"Forget I asked," she said. "None of my business. But why are you here now, in this office? With a hostage no less?"

"Hostage? Oh, you. Right. Well, it wasn't my plan. And it's a long story."

"I've got time. Four hours, apparently, until the current chief arrives."

"Are you the chief's assistant? Is that why you're in his office?"

"Assistant? What makes you think I'm not his boss?"

"Are you?"

She smiled. "No. I'm a crime data analyst. I came in here to print out some reports since my printer's broken. Unfortunately, my timing couldn't have been worse."

"Sorry. Both for the male chauvinist assumption that you were an assistant, and for ruining your day by locking you in here with me."

"Handsome and also able to admit his mistakes when he makes them. Where have you been all my life?"

He couldn't help grinning. "You're cracking jokes while locked in a room with an armed man, twice your size, who's on the run from the police. Are you not intimidated at all?"

"Nope. I've got Wesley."

"Wesley?"

She pulled her hand out from beneath the desk and pointed a pistol at him. "Meet Wesley, otherwise known as a Smith and Wesson M&P9, the best 9mm pistol on the market, in my opinion. Makes that Glock 17 shoved in the small of your back look like a toy."

He slowly raised his hands, the cuffs rattling against each other on his left wrist. "This just keeps getting better and better."

"You probably should have kept your gun out until you were sure that I wasn't armed. You underestimated me."

He couldn't help smiling again, even though his situation was far from amusing. "I guess that goes along with the assistant assumption. What now? You want me to move the filing cabinet?"

"Eventually. Right now I'd appreciate it if you'd scoot away from the desk so my finger doesn't get too itchy on the trigger."

He stepped back several feet. "And I'd appreciate it if you'd move your finger to the gun's frame. At this distance, you can still put it back on the trigger before I could jump you. But it could save my life if you get a muscle spasm in your hand, or just squeeze without thinking about it."

"Good point." She moved her finger. "Better?"

"Yes. Thank you."

"Now take your Glock and pitch it underneath the desk. Slowly."

He did as she asked, then raised his hands again. "What now? You hold the cards."

"I'm debating."

"What are the options?" he asked.

"You tell me. You must have had some kind of plan before you backed in here. What were you going to do?"

Not seeing that it mattered at this juncture, he decided to go with the truth. He moved toward the other side of the room. Her pistol followed his every step. He placed his hand on the wall about six feet up. "I'm going to press this panel. Don't let that trigger finger get itchy."

"I'm as steady as a frog on a lily pad."

"That's what I'm afraid of. Here goes." He pressed the panel and it slid back into the wall, revealing a dark opening behind it.

Her brows raised. "You know about the hidden hallway?"

He frowned. "This isn't a surprise?"

"No. But history was my minor while pursuing my Criminal Justice degree. Specifically, Louisiana history, with a special emphasis on my hometown, Beauchamp. Building architecture is part of that, including all the major landmark buildings, like this one. The hidden hallways with secret panels that open up onto the stairwells are common in a lot of structures around here. Most are marked on the original blueprints, pretty easy to find if you care enough to do a little research. Most people don't."

He looked down the dark hallway. "Most people? Who around here *does* know?"

"Me, obviously. My dad, because I share pretty much everything with him." She tapped her free hand on top of the desk. "Come to think of it, that's probably it."

"Then I don't have to worry about Hank or Gary sneaking up on us?"

"No. You don't."

He stepped closer to the desk, keeping a watchful eye on her pistol as it followed him across the room. "I don't suppose you have a car in the parking garage downstairs and would consider letting me borrow it?"

"I have an SUV, yes. But, no, you may not borrow it."

"Fair enough. Would you consider letting me go? I

could disappear down the hallway and figure out my own transportation once I'm outside the building. You could tell the chief that I pointed my gun at you and you had no choice."

"Hmm. Well, that might be hard to pull off."

"Why is that?"

"Because the chief is standing right behind you."

Mason whirled around. A long gun was aimed directly at his gut by a man nearly as big as him, standing in the opening to the secret hallway.

"Put your hands up, Ford," the man ordered.

Mason slowly raised his hands. "I thought you were in New Orleans."

"I was having breakfast down the street. Al lied."

"You can't trust anyone these days." He glanced over his shoulder. "I'm guessing you lied too, when you said only you and your father knew about this hallway."

"I didn't lie."

"I was *really* hoping you wouldn't say that. The last names—you're married?"

"Widowed." She waved toward the man with the gun. "Former police chief Mason Ford, meet current police chief Mitch Landry. My daddy."

Chapter Four

Hannah returned her gun to her purse as her father yanked Mason's arms behind him and clicked a new pair of handcuffs into place. She winced in sympathy when she saw the wince on Mason's face, quickly hidden. Normally her dad wasn't that rough with prisoners. If anything, he treated them far more politely then they typically deserved. But she supposed he was a bit more aggressive this time because he felt he was protecting his daughter. Then again, maybe it wasn't her father's rough treatment that had caused Mason pain. His face, even one of his hands, had faint bruises, as if he'd recently been in a fight.

"Al told me on the phone how you got away. Pretty neat trick shimming a sunglass arm beneath the ratchets to work that cuff off your wrist," he told Mason. "Never heard of anyone doing that before. I'm going to have to order a different type of handcuff in the future."

"I've got a lot more tricks where that came from. Let me go and I'll be happy to teach you."

"Nice try." He motioned with his long gun toward the secret hallway.

"Daddy, wait. Please."

He held his free hand up, making Mason stop. "I need to get this man to lockup, Hannah. We can talk after."

"I don't want you to lock him up."

Mason looked just as surprised as her father.

She rounded the desk, hesitating when her father angled his body partway between her and Mason.

"Don't get too close," he cautioned. "This guy's a big fellow. Even in restraints, he's dangerous."

Mason nodded, echoing her father's advice. One former chief of police agreeing with the other that she should be more careful around a prisoner. That spoke volumes to Mason's character, not that she needed any proof. She knew all about him, even though this was her first time meeting him.

She leaned back against the front of the desk. "I assume since you called him Mr. Ford when you came in that Al told you who this man is?"

"If you mean a murder suspect, he did. That's why he's going to lockup."

"He used to be the chief of police, the one before that joke, Holloway, came along and undid half the things Mason had done to fix this place."

"I know who he is, Hannah. That doesn't change anything. He was caught holding a gun, trying to leave a murder scene. His ex-fiancée is the one who was shot and killed. Open-and-shut case."

"Open-and-shut." Mason shook his head. "I've heard that before. From the district attorney who helped the mayor and others frame my older brother for murder.

Before I could prove his innocence, he'd been killed in his prison cell. I'm no more guilty of murder than he was. But you'll be just as guilty as the corrupt officials I helped the FBI lock up years ago if you let whoever framed me start this cycle all over again. How long do you think I'll last in a cell? I guarantee I'll never make it to court. Someone went to far too much trouble to get me here to risk what I might uncover in a trial."

Her father's face flushed. "You're missing one critical fact in that speech you just made. *I'm* the chief of police now. And I don't tolerate conspiracies or railroading innocent people into prison. You'll get a fair trial. I'll make sure of it."

In spite of her father's earlier warning, Hannah stepped closer and put her hand on his arm. "Like Julian did?"

His eyes flashed with anger. "I was on vacation when that happened."

Mason glanced back and forth between them. "Who's Julian?"

Hannah waited. She'd thrown down the gauntlet. It was her father's job to pick it up.

He sighed and met Mason's questioning gaze, long gun still pointed at him. "He was the town drunk. Got arrested for a hit-and-run, a little girl. She died. Julian was found the next morning hanging in his cell. Later, we proved he wasn't even involved in the accident."

"Suicide?" Mason asked.

Her father's throat worked. "No."

Mason's eyes widened. "Vigilante justice in Sabine Parish. Again. I see."

"No, you don't see," her father snapped. "That happened a few months after I started as chief. I was still untangling the mess around here because half of *your* deputies had been imprisoned or fired and most of the replacements were pathetic. The city hired an imbecile to replace you and a host of other incompetents after that. I did the best I could at the time, given the situation. The guy who killed Julian is sitting in prison right now, doing life without parole."

"Who killed Julian?"

"One of my father's most trusted deputies." Hannah dropped her hand from her father's arm. "Don't give me that hurt look, Daddy. It's the truth. Yes, you've done a lot to fix the problems around here. But there's a long tradition of corruption in this town, and it will take decades to weed it all out, if it's even possible. Knowing Mason's past, and all the people around here who think of him as their enemy, are you really willing to bet his life that you can protect him if you lock him up here? Look at the bruises on his face. I imagine he's hiding worse ones beneath his suit."

Mason's dark brows arched in surprise. "Observant. I bet you're a great analyst."

"I will be, once I get more experience under my belt. Thanks for the compliment."

"Stop," her father warned. "Quit treating him like a friend instead of a criminal. I'm sure he resisted arrest or he wouldn't have gotten hurt. My deputies don't beat up prisoners."

Mason scoffed.

Her father narrowed his eyes in warning.

Mason directed his next comment to her. "While I appreciate that you want to argue on my behalf, I have to wonder why you're doing it. We don't know each other. Why do you want to help me?"

"I'd like to know that myself," her father said. "What in tarnation is going on here?"

"Olivia."

"My baby sister?" Mason asked.

"Since she's twenty-three, I don't know that *baby* really fits anymore. But, yes. She was one of my best friends in college. And you can get that skeptical look off your face, Mason. I know I'm a lot older than her, but I didn't go to college right after high school, like she did." She waved her hand in the air. "Doesn't matter. Regardless of the age difference, she and I hit it off our freshman year. She was so quiet and, well, seemingly fragile and in need of a friend that I had to introduce myself. I'm exceedingly glad that I did."

He smiled sadly. "Olivia took Landon's death harder than anyone else in the family. She's never gotten over it. *Fragile* is an apt description."

She gave him a sympathetic look. "I was pretty lost myself when we met. My husband died several years ago and I was trying to get my life together and return to the job market. I think Olivia helped me far more than I've ever helped her."

"Sounds like Olivia. She has a good soul and a soft heart." He gave her a sympathetic look. "I'm sorry about your husband."

She nodded her thanks.

"Oh good grief." Her father frowned at both of them.

"Enough already. Hannah, why are you so interested in helping Mr. Ford? You said it had to do with his sister?"

She crossed her arms, unable to hide her irritation with her father. "She's bent my ear many times telling me about her amazing second-oldest brother, who took on the whole town and won. I've heard all kinds of things about his work as well, in Tennessee. He's a good man. The least you can do is give him a few minutes to explain what's happened, from his perspective. Then decide how to proceed."

Her father rolled his eyes. "You'll never let me hear the end of this if I don't, will you?"

"You know I won't."

He motioned toward the desk. "Sit behind that so there's a few more feet between you two and a solid obstacle to slow him down. I'll give him a few minutes to say his piece. *Then* I'm taking him to lockup."

"Thanks, Daddy." She hurried behind the desk and sat. To her surprise, her father uncuffed Mason. Well, he removed *one* of the cuffs, then attached it to the arm of a heavy chair in front of the desk.

Mason's mouth quirked in a wisp of a smile as he rattled the cuff against the chair arm.

Her father sat in a guest chair across from him, but at least he wasn't pointing the long gun anymore. Instead, he had it propped across the two arms of his chair, ready to swing in his direction if needed.

"Don't even think about trying to shim those cuffs off, or breaking the chair arm to escape. I don't care what tricks you think you know. You can't outrun a bullet."

Mason glanced at the gun, then nodded.

"Start talking," her father told him. "And make it fast. Al will buzz my phone soon if I don't check in. I sneaked up that back hallway without telling him I was in the building yet."

"I'll tell you what I know, which isn't much, unfortunately. From what I gather, today's Sunday, right?"

Her father frowned, then nodded.

"Okay, then *yesterday* morning I was in a Gatlinburg, Tennessee, parking lot, surprised to see Audrey Broussard, my former fiancée, standing by my car. She said she wanted another chance at reconciliation. I told her no, as I've done every other time she's come to see me. I went home, was attacked by five masked men in my kitchen and drugged. I specifically remember feeling a needle being jammed into my neck. Next thing I know, I wake up here, in Beauchamp, in a house I've never been in before. Audrey was dead on the floor from a gunshot wound and I was holding a gun. I'm sure once you run ballistics, you'll find the bullet was fired from my pistol."

"Because you shot her."

His eyes glittered with anger. "Because whoever killed her is framing me. And I can tell you the names of two of the men involved. Gary Donnelly and Hank Abrams."

Her father's eyebrows shot up. "Two of my deputies? What are you talking about?"

"They were wearing disguises in my home. But I heard their voices, and one of the other men called them

Hank and Gary. I heard those same voices, and their names again, at the murder scene."

Her father chewed on that for a moment, then said, "First of all, we only have your word that you were attacked and kidnapped. Second, if they wore disguises, you can't identify them. I'm not willing to condemn two of my deputies on something that flimsy. And this whole thing doesn't pass the smell test anyway. If someone wanted to frame you for Ms. Broussard's murder, it would be far simpler to murder her in Gatlinburg, if she was there visiting you. Why go to the trouble of drugging you and transporting you here? It doesn't make sense."

"Sure it does," Mason countered. "I've got a company, friends, allies in Gatlinburg. Here?" He scoffed. "Even my own family won't risk being seen with me. They know all the enemies I've got in Beauchamp, the families of the people sitting in prison because I brought the FBI in here. My enemies will vandalize my family's property and make their lives a living hell. That's the reason I left in the first place. Even after I won my civil suit against the town, the harassment against my family wouldn't stop. Framing me in Gatlinburg? Next to impossible. Framing me here? Slam dunk."

Her father was shaking his head before he finished. "Why frame you at all? And why kill Audrey? You've been in Gatlinburg how many years?"

"My brother was murdered eight years ago. The criminal trial, my subsequent civil trial and the aftermath from it took another year."

"Seven years then, give or take. Did something happen recently to put you on someone's radar back here?"

"Only Audrey visiting. Nothing else that I know of."

"Seven years after you leave, someone, what, finds out Audrey is heading to Gatlinburg to visit you, so they decide to kidnap you, bring you back here, kill her and frame you? If a woman hadn't died, I'd be laughing my head off. The whole thing sounds ridiculous."

Mason's voice was hard as steel when he responded. "So does framing my older brother for shooting his girlfriend. And yet, here we are. Same town. Same setup. Different victims."

"All the people behind your brother's frame-up went to prison a long time ago."

"Not all of them. The real murderer was never caught. No one would roll over and give up his name. Everyone who went to prison was part of the FBI corruption investigation I headed. The only way I could get any kind of justice for what happened to my brother was through the civil lawsuit. No one ever did time for what happened to him, or to Mandy DuBois, his girlfriend. That's a cold case. And from what I've seen, no one here is even trying to solve it."

Her father's face turned red. "It's still an open case. But there has to be new evidence to lead in a new direction or there's no point in having someone working it."

"Have you even *read* the case files?"

"As I said earlier, I've been working on cleaning up the mess that still remains from after you left and the new mayor appointed a string of idiots to replace you.

Working your brother's and Ms. DuBois's cases hasn't been a priority. I'm sorry, but that's the way it is."

Hannah held her hands up. "Can we lower the temperature in here a few degrees and get back to Mason's predicament?"

"Predicament?" Her father's voice was just as hard as Mason's. "He's been arrested for murder and needs to be locked up. Nothing I've heard changes that. Why would a killer, a full eight years after the original murder, decide to do the exact same crime all over again to the brother of the man he originally framed?"

"Maybe it's not the same killer," Mason snapped. "Maybe he's a copycat. How am I supposed to know?"

"I don't think either of you are asking the right questions," Hannah said. "Yes, if killing Mason was the primary goal, or the only goal, then killing him in Tennessee makes sense. But the person who orchestrated his kidnapping had to gain something by bringing Mason here and framing him for Audrey's murder. What does he gain?"

"That's easy," Mason said. "He humiliates my family, and me, once again. It took years for my family to live down the notoriety of everything that happened. Now all of that will be rehashed and my family will likely be harassed again."

"Someone has a vendetta against you, your family, or both. Maybe they have a vendetta against Audrey too, and once they realized she was going to visit you, they used that to their advantage."

Her father gave her a long look, then shrugged.

"Makes a little more sense. But who hates Mason and Audrey enough to do all that?"

"What about her most recent fiancé?" Hannah asked. "Wasn't Richard Thibodeaux your best friend, Mason?"

"A long time ago, yes."

"He broke up with Audrey and left town. Maybe she brought your name up one too many times and he felt threatened. Maybe he blames you for destroying their relationship and wanted revenge on both of you."

Mason shook his head. "Richard would never do that. I've known him most of my life. Yes, Audrey played us against each other and destroyed our friendship. But that didn't make us enemies. We both moved on, moved forward. As for Audrey, she could be…difficult, when she didn't get her way. She had her share of altercations with people in town. But I can't think of anyone who actually hated her, or wanted to hurt her. As for my enemies, the list is too long to contemplate. Half the town resents me or blames me for the people who went to prison and the payout the town had to do in my civil case. The fact that the town's insurance company covered the judgment doesn't seem to matter to anyone. They take it personally that I sued Beauchamp."

"Is there a point to any of this?" her father asked. "It's all speculation. The simplest explanation, the most obvious, is that Audrey humiliated Mr. Ford in Tennessee and he wanted revenge. Or, heck, maybe she was blackmailing you. There are rumors that you're a wealthy man, that you've grown that civil suit money into a heck of a lot more than you started out with. Is that true?"

Mason gave him a crisp nod.

"What if Audrey has something on you and threatened your financial empire? And you felt you had no choice but to stop her, for good?"

"Since I offered her money in Gatlinburg, and she turned me down, that pretty much eliminates a blackmail angle."

"So you say."

Mason's fingers gripped the chair arms so tightly his knuckles whitened.

Her father, likewise, tightened his grip on the long gun resting across his chair arms. "I still say that you followed her here and killed her."

"I don't even know where she lives these days."

"That's hard to believe since you were found in her house."

Mason swore. "That's news to me. And I've already told you, I wasn't there of my own accord. I was drugged and kidnapped and brought here against my will."

"Or you followed her from Gatlinburg."

"You're kidding, right?" Mason gave him an incredulous look. "How could I follow her all the way from Tennessee to Louisiana without her losing me along the way? Or spotting me in her rearview mirror? Talk about far-fetched."

"Maybe you put some kind of tracking device on her car."

"Right. She shows up unannounced, confronts me in a parking lot with my whole company watching, and I happen to have a tracking device handy and put it on her car? And no one notices? How far down this rabbit hole do you want to go to make your version hold water?"

"I'm just throwing out hypotheticals. Whether I'm right or wrong about any of it doesn't even matter. The truth will come out during the investigation. In the meantime, there was plenty of probable cause for your arrest. And you can sit in jail like anyone else until you either make bail, or the judge denies bail and you wait until this thing goes to trial." He stood and worked on the cuff attached to Mason's chair.

Hannah shoved to her feet. "How was the arrest made? Mason, what happened, specifically?"

Mason stood and turned around so her father could cuff his arms behind his back.

"Mason?" she pushed. "What happened?"

Her father stepped back, cradling his gun in his arms. At least he wasn't pointing it at Mason. Yet. "Go on. Might as well finish."

It took a few moments for Mason to answer. He seemed to be struggling to tamp down his anger. She couldn't blame him for being angry. She'd be furious if she was in his situation. As much as she loved and respected her father, she was certain that this time he was wrong. Of course she had the advantage of hearing for years about the good work Mason had done, both here and in Tennessee after starting some kind of company that helped people in need, regardless of their ability to pay.

When his dark gaze finally met hers, the anger was still there, but tightly leashed. He was like a caged tiger, ready to explode, but determined not to vent his frustration at her.

"When I woke up this morning and realized I wasn't in my own house, I instinctively reached for my gun. It just happened to be sitting on the bedside table. That was a huge red flag and I knew I was in trouble. I had to get out of the house before whoever was plotting against me came back. I rushed downstairs. Then I saw Audrey." Pain flashed in his eyes but was quickly hidden. "As soon as I recovered from that shock, the police were busting down the door and arresting me."

"I'm sorry about Audrey," she said.

His jaw tightened and he gave her a crisp nod.

"You said the police arrived as soon as you found her. How did they know to go there?" she asked.

"Al said there was a 911 call," her father chimed in.

Hannah stared at her father. "And you don't find that strange? Given the circumstances? Where did the call come from?"

He pursed his lips. "It was anonymous."

She crossed her arms. "No kidding. Wasn't the 911 call with his brother's frame-up also anonymous?"

Her father's face reddened again. "I'm not familiar enough with that case to say."

Mason's gaze flashed to her father but he didn't say anything. Maybe he didn't see the point of arguing anymore since her father still wasn't backing down.

Pounding sounded on the door to the office. "The chief's closer than I thought, " Al yelled. "He'll be here soon. Why don't you open up and we'll wait for him together?"

A few seconds later, her father's phone buzzed in his pocket. He checked the screen. "Al's asking where I am. Says he's ready to bust down the door. He's tired of waiting and he's gambling you won't actually shoot anyone."

"Dad, you have to help Mason, give him a fighting chance. Do you really want to risk another Julian?"

He frowned. "That's a low blow."

"I know. I'm sorry. But I can't imagine with your sense of fair play that you aren't wondering whether this is a frame-up. Can you really be certain no one will harm him if he's locked up?"

The door rattled again as something hit it.

Her father looked at Mason, then shook his head in exasperation. "Go on, Ford. Stall him. I'll text Al that I got waylaid downstairs taking care of a problem, that I'll be up soon."

Mason hesitated, glancing at her father's gun as if he didn't trust him.

He pointed it toward the floor. "I'm not going to shoot you unless you give me a good reason to. Go on."

Mason crossed the room and yelled through the door, telling Al to give him more time.

Hannah smiled. "Thank you, Daddy."

"You misunderstand. He's going to jail. I just want a few more minutes to wrap my head around this, get as much information as I can."

"One phone call can straighten all of this out." Mason stopped a yard away from her father.

"You can call your lawyer after you're booked."

"I'm not talking about a lawyer. I mean my team, The Justice Seekers."

"The what?"

"My company, in Gatlinburg. We perform investigations and offer protection to those who've run into hard times, when conventional avenues haven't worked out."

"Conventional avenues? You mean the law?" He sounded derisive. "You protect *criminals*?"

Mason's eyes looked cold enough to freeze her father in his tracks. "We help *innocent people* who can't get what they need through normal channels. Like abused women and children. I can get one of my men to check the security system at my house and prove I was kidnapped. That should go a long way toward establishing reasonable doubt about my guilt."

"Even if what you say is true, I can't imagine a group of five guys going after you without looking for something like security cameras and taking them out, first thing. I doubt there's any video to see."

"They wouldn't have seen the cameras. They're hidden, outside on the property and inside the house. The electronic feed goes straight to the network at Camelot."

"Camelot? What the heck are you talking about now?"

He sighed heavily. "My company's headquarters."

"Are all rich people as eccentric as you?"

Mason's eyes flashed with anger again.

Her father's hold on his long gun never wavered. There was no sign of him giving in. "If you've got a camera system that fancy, you must have an alarm. And yet you said they surprised you."

"You're right. My alarm should have sent a text to my watch when they broke in." He held up his right wrist, showing them the watch in question, a sleek black band so thin it looked more like a bracelet than a watch.

"There was no text. All I can figure is those men knew how to disarm the system. Just call my company. Get them to check the server. They can log in remotely, get the security feed within minutes and send it right to your phone."

"Daddy—"

"All right, all right. You've got me curious. I don't see where a phone call can hurt. Who will I be talking to?"

"Bishop." He rattled off the number as her father punched it into his phone.

"Just *Bishop*? Is that his first name or last?"

"It's what he'll answer to."

Her father mumbled something again about eccentrics, then spoke into the phone when someone answered. A few moments later, he and Mason were both bent over the phone's screen, watching the security recording, while Hannah leaned as far over the desk as her father would allow so she could see it too.

She sucked in a shocked breath, watching the proof of everything Mason had said. Masked men swarmed an incredibly upscale kitchen, punching, kicking and jumping on Mason. If there'd been one less of them, they might not have won. He was holding his own amazingly well against such overwhelming odds. But the bad guys eventually got him on the floor, and just as he'd described, one of them jabbed a needle into his neck. He went limp, his eyes closing.

"Son of a gun," her father said. "You weren't lying. Any idea who the one guy was talking about when he said some woman wanted you taken alive?"

"I'd forgotten about that. But when he said it, I wondered whether Audrey was mad at me for turning her down and hired someone to beat me up. It feels disloyal even saying that. She was never violent. It's just as likely that someone's mad that my company helped put one of their loved ones in prison and wants me to suffer, at Audrey's expense."

"Maybe." Her father didn't sound convinced. Neither did Mason.

"Your guy, Bishop, just texted me another link, said it's from the outside of your house, before the guys broke in." He clicked it, then held the screen up for all of them to watch the next video.

A dark-colored SUV drove up the driveway.

"Dad, isn't that a Ford Expedition? Like Audrey Broussard owns?"

"I thought she drove a red convertible."

"So did I," Mason said. "That's what she's always driven. It's what she had in the Gatlinburg parking lot when she spoke to me."

"She's got two cars. I only know because I was at the dealership a few months ago getting my Tucson serviced and saw her buying the Expedition. Like you, I was surprised and asked her if she was trading in her convertible. She said no, but that she needed something bigger for her interior decorating business to carry samples."

"Since when did she have her own business?" her

father asked. "I thought she lived off investments and money from the guys she dated." He shot a glance at Mason. "No offense."

Mason's mouth tilted in a wry smile. "None taken."

Hannah shrugged. "I'd heard she'd started up some kind of business early this year but didn't press for details. We were friendly, saw each other around town on occasion. But I wouldn't call us friends."

Mason nodded toward the paused video. "If that is her SUV, I don't know what to make of it. Maybe she'd hired men here and had them drive up with her. She planned to have me brought to her home, thinking she could try again to convince me to stay with her."

"After having some guys beat you up?" Hannah shook her head. "I can't imagine anyone thinking that was a good way to restart a relationship."

"Honestly, I'm grasping at straws right now. I don't know what to think."

"It's a common enough type of vehicle," her father said. "Doesn't mean it's hers. Let's watch the rest of the video."

Five men exited the SUV. But the driver stayed inside, dark-tinted windows and the camera angle protecting his, or her, identity. The group of men headed around the back of the house, their movements picked up by yet another camera. Three wore masks, two carried them in their hands. The reason soon became clear. They must not have wanted their masks to obscure their vision as they performed the meticulous task of disabling the security system. Once that was done, they both turned toward the house and raised their masks, but not before the camera got a perfect shot.

It was Abrams and Donnelly.

Mason didn't seem surprised.

Her father looked shocked, and obviously furious. He stopped the video, his mouth clamped so tight his lips formed a hard line.

"Dad? Are you okay?"

"No, Hannah. I am *not* okay. Give me a minute. Just one dang minute. I have to think." He shook his head a few moments later. "That explains the alarm not going off. Abrams used to work for an alarm company. Knows every kind of system on the market, backward and forward. He and Donnelly are bosom buddies. Must have taught him everything he knew. That rat-faced jerk."

A faint knock sounded through the office door again. "What's going on in there?" Al's muffled voice called out. "Open this door, Chief Ford."

Her father put his phone away. "This is a hell of a mess. I don't know who to trust anymore. I knew I'd coddled Abrams and Donnelly too dang much. But the pickins' are slim around here with the pathetic salaries the city pays deputies, and no compensation for overtime. I pretty much hired anyone who'd agree to the pay scale. Still, with all the issues those two have with everyone else on the team, I should have dug deeper, should have realized they were dirty and canned them both long ago."

Mason shook his head. "Half my police force was on the take for years, and I didn't know. This isn't on you. It's on them. Don't blame yourself."

He eyed Mason. "How many years did it take you to not blame yourself?"

Mason didn't answer.

"That's what I thought. Here you are trying to console me and you still blame yourself." He rubbed the back of his neck. "The buck stops here, don't it? A chief is always responsible for the actions of his men." He lowered the long gun so the muzzle was pointed at the floor. "If I let you go, do you have someplace you can lie low, where no one will think to look? Not with family either. That's the first place anyone would search."

Mason's brows shot up. "I've got a cottage a block from the historic district that I bought not too long ago. It's probably six blocks from here, listed under an alias that I created for my occasional trips down here."

"That won't work. It's way too close to the station and we patrol the historic district more heavily than the rest of town because of all the tourists. The chances of being spotted are too high."

"Before I bought the house, I stayed at a place I own north of town. It's in a rural area. Secluded. No neighbors. And the deed is buried under a maze of shell companies, so it won't come up on a property search as belonging to me."

"No one around here knows you own it? Family? Friends?"

"No one *anywhere* knows I own it. I don't come to Beauchamp to socialize. I come to work on my brother's case."

The implied insult—that no one else was working

on his brother's case—seemed to hang in the room. But her father ignored it. "How far out are we talking?"

"Ten miles, give or take."

He scrubbed his jaw. "That might work, at least for the short term. What about transportation? How will you get there?"

"I'll figure something out."

Her father shook his head. "Not good enough. You need to disappear and I need to know you're safe. I won't have your murder on my conscience."

"I can drive him where he needs to go." Hannah grabbed her keys and slung her purse over her shoulder. "We'll open the window and make it look like he jumped out and got away. The facade is covered with clinker bricks. They stick out every foot or so, like little stepping-stones. Someone desperate enough could use them to scale the wall. In theory, at least. It's a believable scenario. The three of us can head down the back hallway so no one learns about the secret passageway. When Al breaks the door down, he'll find an empty room and an open window. He'll assume Mason climbed out. Then you'll come up in the elevator to handle things while Mason and I are getting out of Dodge."

Her father stared at her, eyes wide. "When did my crime analyst turn into a criminal mastermind?"

"Not criminal, Daddy. Just a mastermind." She smiled.

Her father shook his head, but returned her smile.

Al banged on the door, louder this time. "You've got one minute, Ford. Then we're coming in whether you want us to or not. And if you shoot at us, we'll blow this door to bits, you right along with it."

"Mason," her father said, dropping the Mr. Ford formality. "The bruises. Did my men do that when they arrested you?"

"No, sir. Your men showed remarkable restraint at the murder scene. They followed protocol. My bruises are from when I was attacked at my home."

Her father gave him a grateful nod, relief palpable on his face. "Hannah, how sure are you that Olivia's right, that Mason's really a good man?"

Mason's gaze shot to hers.

"One hundred percent. If we had time, I'd tell you the stories about his bravery, and how he's helped save dozens of lives, including those of many of the people working for him. He's a good man, Daddy. The best. I know it."

Mason's eyes closed briefly, and he let out a ragged breath, as if in relief.

"Let me do this, Daddy. I'll drop him off and come right back. No one will even know I helped him. Please. If you turn him over, it'll be like when his brother was arrested all those years ago. Or when Julian was arrested."

Pain flashed in his eyes, which had her feeling horrible. But a man's life was on the line. She'd do whatever it took to make her father see reason.

He cleared his throat. "You'll come right back?"

"Promise."

"All right. Open the window. Hurry."

She rushed to the window, unlocked it, then shoved

it up. When she turned around, Mason—no longer in handcuffs—was standing by her father at the entrance to the secret passageway. She hurried over to them.

"Al doesn't bluff," her father said. "He's going to bust in that door. Let's get you two out of here. I'll do what my daughter suggested, head up in the elevator and pretend like I just got freed up from some crisis downstairs. I'll buy you some time. Hannah, call me when you get wherever you're going. Don't tell me where you're at. But call me. Then get back here as soon as you can."

"Will do." She kissed his cheek. "I love you, Daddy."

He gave her a curt nod, which meant more to her than anyone else's proclamation of love.

The three of them stepped into the hidden passageway. Her father sealed the entrance just as a loud noise sounded from the office. True to his word, Al was breaking down the door.

They took off running.

Chapter Five

Mason hopped into the front passenger seat of Hannah's dark blue Tucson, barely getting his door shut before she took off through the parking garage.

"Easy," he said. "We don't want to attract attention. Let's go the speed limit, okay? We'll be long gone before Al can bust in past that filing cabinet and discover I escaped."

"Right. Sorry." She slowed down to the five miles per hour posted in the garage. At the end of the row, she headed toward the exit, glancing down each side aisle as she went.

A shadow moved off to their right. "Stop!" Mason yelled.

She slammed her brakes, skidding to a halt about ten feet from the man who'd led the arrest brigade against Mason. Captain Murphy. He stood in the middle of the lane, legs braced wide apart, both hands clasped around the pistol he was aiming at Mason.

"Out of the vehicle, Ford. Keep your hands where I can see them."

Mason swore. "I knew this was going too well." He reached for the door handle.

"Hang on." Hannah slammed the accelerator.

The Tucson jumped forward, throwing Mason back against the seat.

Murphy dived to the side, rolling out of the way to avoid being hit. She blew past him through the exit, out onto the street. Horns blared. A car swerved, narrowly missing her. She screeched around the corner, then headed north through town.

"Hannah, you almost ran over a policeman. We need to pull over and de-escalate what's about to become a very dangerous situation."

"I would have swerved if he hadn't jumped out of the way." She slowed, but only to check both ways at a stop sign, before speeding through the intersection.

"This escape attempt was over the moment Murphy saw me. We need to stop, call the police and let me turn myself in. I'll tell them I saw you in the garage and tried to steal your car. You pulled your gun and I got it away from you, then held you at gunpoint. But after I forced you to speed out of the garage, almost hitting Murphy, you convinced me to give myself up. You'll be in the clear."

"I'm not letting you turn yourself in."

Sirens sounded in the distance. Either Murphy, or Al, or both had alerted patrol. He looked through the rear window but didn't see any flashing lights. Yet.

The SUV bounced over potholes and careened around another corner. He grabbed the armrest to keep from being thrown against the door. A quick glance at Hannah told him they were in trouble. Stress lines creased the corners of her eyes and she seemed on the verge of hyperventilating.

"Hannah." He tried to make his voice sound soothing. "I need you to slow down. Ease off the gas."

"Can't. Don't you hear them? They're not far behind." She bit her lip and checked the mirrors.

The wobble in her voice wasn't reassuring with her bumping through narrow residential streets and weaving around parked cars.

"Hannah?" When she didn't answer, he said it more softly. "Hannah?"

She frowned and weaved around another car.

Ever so carefully, he feathered his fingers down her cheek, then pressed the back of his hand against the side of her neck. "Hannah? Take a breath. In, out. Look at me for just a second."

She blinked as if coming out of a trance and shot him a glance. "Y-yes?"

"This looks like a family neighborhood. What if a little kid runs out from behind one of those cars?"

She blinked again, then reduced her speed. "Thanks." Her voice sounded hoarse. She cleared it and tried again. "I didn't think about that." She flexed her hands against the steering wheel.

He let out a relieved breath. She'd calmed down, at least a little, and was driving more carefully. He'd still prefer she slow down more, or pull over. But he'd made some progress. "Up ahead, on the right. That looks like a good place to pull over."

Her brows drew down in a frown. "You're giving me tone."

"Tone?"

"Your voice. It's the way your brother Wyatt talks to Olivia when she's gone off her medication or hits a rough patch. I'm not having a psychotic break. I'm just…a little nervous, okay?" She shot him an aggravated look. "I'm trying to save your life. Everything I've heard about you tells me it's a life worth saving. So how about instead of fighting me, you help me."

"I *am* trying to help. Don't throw away the years of hard work you've put into going back to college and starting a brand-new career as a crime data analyst."

She winced.

"Stop the car. I'll surrender. You're the innocent victim I took at gunpoint. This all goes away."

"For me. Not for you! The DA will tack kidnapping onto your other charges. That's federal, with big-time penalties. I'm not going to lie and say you forced me into helping you escape. That would make me as bad as whoever killed Audrey and framed you. I'd rather rot in jail than face myself in the mirror every day knowing I traded your life to get myself out of trouble."

"Let's say we manage to outrun them. Then what?"

"I thought you said you had a place north of town where we could hide out."

"I do. But *you* have a *life*, here, in Beauchamp. A career. I never planned on you staying with me. *Neither did your father*. You promised him you'd drop me off and go right back. He wouldn't want you to do this."

She swallowed hard. Was he finally getting through to her?

"Daddy will understand. I'll stay with you, for now. My life will be waiting for me after this is over."

Apparently he *hadn't* gotten through to her. "Not if you're charged with a felony, aiding and abetting a fugitive."

"I'm helping an innocent man. It will all work out. But not if they kill you like they did your brother."

He shook his head, both impressed and appalled by her naivete. He'd been idealistic once too, believing justice would always prevail. But he'd learned that right didn't always triumph over wrong.

She headed up a straightaway, leaving the neighborhoods behind and entering a more rural, sparsely populated area. "Should I keep going north? You said ten miles, right?"

"Give or take."

"Help me, Mason. Us getting caught won't fix this. I'm not going to lie when they ask me what happened."

"What about your dad? Will you tell them he let me go? At best, it would destroy his career. At worst, he'll face charges."

She drew a shaky breath. "He'll do what works for his conscience. I'll do what works for mine. Where's your hideout?"

"Are you always this stubborn?"

"If an innocent person's life is at stake, you'd better believe it."

He couldn't help smiling. "You sound like one of my Justice Seekers."

"There you go. I can work for you when this is over. Maybe not as a crime analyst. But I can put my criminal justice degree to good use helping in some other way. Problem solved."

"Hannah—"

"Where to, Mason? Where's the hideout?"

"Good grief. You're like a dog with a bone."

"Not exactly flattering."

"An intelligent and extremely attractive woman with a favorite gun she named Wesley?"

She smiled. "Much better. Which way?"

He settled back against the seat, conceding. For now. "Highway 191."

Moments later, she zoomed up an access road and swerved onto 191, heading north, almost slamming into the side of a semi blowing its air horn at them.

"My bad." She waved at the trucker before zipping past and speeding down the highway.

When Mason could breathe normally again, he released his death grip on the armrest. "Where'd you learn to drive? NASCAR?"

"Pfft. NASCAR's got nothing on me. I was the local drag racing champion before I turned eleven."

"You say that like it's a good thing."

She grinned, which had him feeling infinitely better. She'd seemed so lost earlier. But the farther they got from town, the more twisty the road became, the less stressed she seemed. Her mood had definitely lightened and she seemed more like the flirty, fun woman he'd pegged her to be when he'd barricaded himself in her father's office.

A siren whined somewhere behind them again. She glanced in the rearview mirror. "Dang it. Someone must have called in about my high-speed jaunt through town."

"Or that semi driver reported a Tucson driving reck-lessly down the highway."

She grinned again, enjoying this mad dash far too much. "Maybe. Either way, I think they've figured out where we are, or at least what road we're on."

"Last chance. Are you sure you want to do this?"

"Really? You're going there again?"

"Apparently not. First, we need to toss your phone. Murphy's probably already putting a trace on it. When the phone's in motion, even if you're not using it, it pings off the cell towers and—"

She threw her phone out the window, then rolled it back up.

He blinked in surprise. "I figured I'd have to argue with you."

"I'm a reasonable person." She glanced at him. "Don't give me that look. Turning you in wasn't a rea-sonable request. Throwing out my phone so they can't track us makes sense. What's next?"

"Get off the highway. There should be a turnoff a couple of miles ahead that we can—"

"Hold on."

He braced his hands against the dash right before she slammed her brakes. She jerked the wheel hard left and went bouncing down a curvy dirt road that seemed to miraculously appear in between thick pines and bushes that scraped the sides of the SUV.

"Or we can take this one," he said drily. He checked

to make sure she had her seat belt fastened. Then he grabbed his own and clicked it in place. As they rounded a curve, he was relieved to see the highway disappear in his side view mirror. And even though he could still hear sirens, they were fading. "Where does this road go?"

"Don't know. Never even noticed it before."

He shook his head, finding it impossible not to smile at her enthusiasm. "What happened to the scared woman from just a few minutes ago? You're actually enjoying this now, aren't you?"

"*Scared* might be a little too harsh. I was…cautious, not used to running from the police, or such high stakes. And, yes, this is the kind of driving I like best. Get me on a Gator or a dune buggy and you'll have to peel me off."

Another jolting bounce had the top of his head brushing the roof. "If you don't slow down, you may have to peel *me* off the roof. Besides, we don't know how long this road is or how quickly it might end."

"You had to say that. Hold on." She slammed the brakes.

They slid toward a stand of thick pines marking the end of the road. Just when it seemed they were about to test out the airbags, she slammed the accelerator and jerked the steering wheel. The Tucson fishtailed and shot to the right, its rear bumper banging against one of the trees before they rocketed a few feet down into what appeared to be a dry creek bed.

Except there weren't any dry creek beds around here,

not with the high water table and bayous surrounding the area.

It must have been another access road to someone's acreage at one time. The waist-high weeds and small saplings she was plowing through attested to its disuse. He studied the woods zipping past the window.

She bounced in a deep rut, making everything squeak.

He winced, his battered body feeling the abuse just as heavily as the Tucson. "I suppose I'll have to buy you a new SUV when this is over."

"Honey, you can buy me anything you want. A new Tucson will do, with all the goodies. Oh, and a phone. Don't forget the phone."

"With all the goodies?"

"Of course."

He laughed. "You got it."

The creek bed, or forgotten access road, ended and they were suddenly in the woods with no obvious path. She was forced to slow even more, picking her way around trees, fallen logs, and occasionally mowing down thick bushes blocking their way.

About ten minutes later, he glimpsed a bog. Flashes of white were probably snowy egrets, which were common around here.

His watch vibrated against his wrist. He glanced at the screen, then looked out the window and saw a blue stripe painted about ten feet up on a pine tree.

"I still hear sirens," she said. "Faint, but definitely sirens. Off to the east I think."

"The highway. It's running roughly parallel to us. I

don't think they found where we turned off or they'd be on our bumper by now."

"If they were, I sure couldn't outrun them. We could probably go faster walking at this point. Maybe we should ditch my car."

"I don't think we'll have to do that."

"Why do you say that?"

"Because I see a building through those trees."

She frowned, then nodded when she saw what he'd told her about. They bounced up a slight incline on their right to get around a fallen log. When she came around the other side, they were in a large clearing that could have held a dozen cars if it was a parking lot. She stopped about twenty feet from the building, a dilapidated-looking barn whose sagging roof seemed ready to collapse in a stiff breeze.

Thick woods surrounded the barn. Through a gap in the trees on the left, sunlight sparkled off brackish water, revealing the bayou he'd spotted earlier. It was dotted with swamp tupelo trees and bald cypress draped in Spanish moss. There would be lily pads and duck-weed too, although he couldn't see them from here. Even with the car door closed and the windows up, the damp mustiness of the bayou drifted in through the air vents.

An unexpected pang of longing settled over him as he drank it all in. In Gatlinburg he'd have a coat on right now. Here, he could wear short sleeves just about year-round. Tennessee was glorious with its seasonal colors, waterfalls that could take his breath away, mist-covered mountains outside his back door. But there was something about the bayous of Louisiana, the music, the food, that tugged at his heart. Even with the horrors that had happened to him and his family in Beauchamp, his blood hummed with pleasure at being in this unique brand of paradise again. It was, quite simply, home.

Hannah thumped the steering wheel in frustration. "The good news is that I think we lost them. I don't hear any sirens. The bad news is I got *us* lost in the process. I don't even know if I can backtrack at this point. I had to make so many turns to get around obstacles. I have no idea where we are."

"About a mile from Pete's Bog. The Sabine River is to the west just past the bayou, maybe a quarter mile as the eagle flies. Highway 191's five miles to the east."

Her brows arched in surprise. "How do you know all that?"

"Because I own that barn and the forty acres surrounding it. Welcome to my hideout."

Chapter Six

As barns went, the one that Hannah was standing in took the prize as the worst she'd ever been inside. Not that she'd been in many. But there were enough of these antiques still around that she'd explored a few, mostly as a teenager up to no good. Unlike this one, though, none of those had seemed ready to fall down. If it wasn't for Mason assuring her this building was far more solid than it looked, she wouldn't have parked her Tucson inside. And she wouldn't be here in the shadows with twenty-foot-tall stacks of moldy hay surrounding her.

"You don't look impressed."

She turned at the sound of his humor-filled voice as he finished securing the massive, sagging doors behind them. "I think the hay bales are the only things holding this place up. I suppose that could be called impressive."

He grinned but remained standing by the doors. "That's all you see? Hay bales?"

She turned in a slow circle, trying to make out details in an interior lit only by what little sun could filter through the small, dirty windows set high up in the walls. "I see dirt floors, dry-rotted walls and rafters, hay that should have been thrown out months or years ago. Not that I'm complaining, since no one would ever think to look for us here. But, well, okay, yes. I'm complaining. It would be nice if it was a whole lot cleaner. As it is, we'll probably have to sleep in my car. And I'm not looking forward to using the woods as an outhouse, or hunting squirrels for dinner." She squinted up at the crisscross of cracked, weathered beams holding up the rusty metal roof. "Are you *sure* this thing isn't going to crash down on top of us?"

"This building is only about six years old."

"You're kidding. What happened to it?"

He laughed. "It was designed to *look* like it should be condemned. The actual bones of the structure are made of steel, set in concrete footers. The rotting wood is for aesthetics, so no one finds this place and starts asking questions about a pristine new building in the middle of nowhere. Even if a hunter or fisherman got curious and broke in, they wouldn't think there was anything of value in here. But they'd be wrong." He winked and stretched his arm up to press a board on the wall. A click sounded. Then a low mechanical hum filled the barn.

That wink had her stomach doing flip-flops. Which was ridiculous. It wasn't like he was flirting with her. He was just being charming, trying to put her at ease. Like when she'd been on the brink of a nervous breakdown trying to evade the police on her wild ride through town. He'd gently touched her face and spoken in that deep, soothing voice—centering her, grounding her, giving her an anchor to bring her back from the edge.

Anyone else with his physical presence—tall, broad-shouldered with biceps that strained against his suit jacket—might have intimidated her. But she'd respected and admired this man's character long before she'd ever met him. And it didn't hurt that his exquisitely handsome face could have been designed by Michelangelo. To top it all off, he was wearing a business suit. How sexy was that?

"Are you impressed now?" he asked, as he stepped beside her.

Her face heated. Had she said all of that out loud?

He motioned toward the back of the barn. She turned, then stared in amazement. "Looks like at least half the hay has been moved on the right side of the building. Wait, is that…is that a door?"

"It is. The first three levels of bales have swung back to reveal the true beauty of this place—a hidden door that leads to a hidden room. Even the ceiling is concealed. If someone climbs into the loft and looks down, all they'll see is hay. And if anyone crosses onto the property, I'll be notified. The boundaries are marked with blue paint on some of the trees. Motion-activated cameras hidden in those trees will send a text to my watch, including pictures, so I can see whether it's someone trespassing or just wildlife."

"Sounds like you thought of everything."

"Not everything. I never expected someone to drive in from the south when the only paved access is on the north side of the property. It took me a while to realize that so-called road we were on was taking us here."

She followed him to the door and motioned toward

the left side of the barn. "The bales on that side haven't moved. Is there a hidden room over there too?"

"Something like that. I'll show you later." He pushed open the door and waited for her to enter.

It was dark, which had her worried about creepy crawlies skittering across her shoes. But she gathered her courage and stepped inside. After the door clicked closed, another click sounded. Light filled the space, revealing a pristine, white room with polished concrete floors. It was long and narrow, maybe thirty by fifteen feet.

She glanced up. Modern canned lights were recessed into the smooth white ceiling. A row of neat, open shelves ran along the left wall, holding a few boxes of nonperishable foods, medicines and a couple of cases of bottled water. There were stacks of electronics, as well. She spotted some phones, at least two laptops. Beneath all that was a long black counter with an assortment of mini kitchen appliances, including a microwave and a beverage cooler.

The end of the room formed the main living area. It boasted a surprisingly large, U-shaped sectional that looked custom-made for the space, with built-ins on the wall above it providing even more storage. A coffee table with a stack of place mats indicated it did double duty as a dining table.

"Dinner might be boring tonight, but you won't go hungry. No need to hunt for squirrels," he teased as he grabbed two bottles of water from the cooler and a bottle of pain pills from one of the shelves.

He handed her one of the water bottles while he washed down several pills.

"Those jerks really did a number on you in Gatlinburg. How bad does it hurt?" She took a deep sip from her own bottle, surprised at how thirsty she was. Apparently fleeing from the police did that to a person.

He set his bottle on the counter. "A good night's sleep will do wonders. But the pills are a welcome crutch for now. What do you think about the place?"

She set her bottle beside his. "I'm honestly impressed. But why buy a house in town if you already had this place? Especially since it had to cost a small fortune to build."

"I come to Beauchamp once or twice a year to research my brother's case. Originally, I used this barn as my home base, with the goal of staying out of town as much as possible. I didn't want to rub salt in old wounds, or upset my family. But even though I was discreet about meeting with potential witnesses, I found most weren't willing to disclose much information. My investigation stalled. For the last few years, I've been working on a new approach. I hired a movie makeup artist to design a reusable disguise. And I created an alias, with a background that could withstand most internet and basic database searches, along with ID that matched my new name, Christopher Johnson."

"Christopher's fairly common around here. Johnson isn't."

"I was going for a Tennessee name. My alias background is from there."

"Good choice then. I'm guessing with the alias and

disguise, you felt comfortable buying the cottage, living in town thinking no one would recognize you?"

"Exactly. You'd be amazed how many people will gossip with a tourist on a hunting or fishing trip, especially if he invested in the community by purchasing a home. It's slow going, getting people to trust and open up. But things are definitely working better with an alias than without one. I've got high hopes something will break loose in the near future." He made a face. "Correction, I *had* high hopes. Who knows what will happen now."

"I just hate that you and your family have suffered the way you have. It's so unfair."

He shrugged. "It is what it is." He reached above the counter and pressed a button on a small electronic keypad she hadn't noticed earlier.

She glanced around, expecting one of the walls to move. "I think something's broken. Nothing's happening."

"The stacks of hay are moving into position outside this room to conceal the door."

"I don't hear the mechanical hum."

"Soundproofing. No sense in having a secret room if someone outside can hear us in here."

"Makes sense. This would be a perfect little apartment if it had windows. But even without natural light, everything's so bright and looks so clean."

"Even with constant ventilation and climate control, it gets pretty dusty between visits. But I was here not long ago, which is why it looks presentable right now. That door over there is the bathroom, with a stackable washer and dryer. That'll come in handy tonight. You can wear my robe or something else from the closet in there while we wash your clothes. It's not ideal, but at least you'll have something clean to wear."

She nodded, but her body flushed with delicious heat thinking about wearing something he'd worn. She cleared her throat. "What about door number two over there? Bedroom?"

"Mechanical room. Houses all the high-tech gizmos that make this place work. I won't bore you with too many details, but the air-conditioning, heating, even the motor for the concealment system is in there with special ventilation and more soundproofing. We've got internet too, with a state-of-the-art fire wall to protect the connection. The satellite dish is camouflaged at the top of a pine tree."

"But no bedroom."

"No bedroom. I didn't see the point in wasting valuable square footage when I can sleep on the couch. But don't worry. I'll take the floor tonight. There's extra bedding in the bathroom closet."

She rolled her eyes. "No way. That sectional is plenty big enough for both of us. I wouldn't dream of letting you sleep on that hard concrete floor, especially with all those bruises."

His eyes widened, but he didn't argue. From the way her pulse was speeding up at the prospect of sleeping so close to him, maybe she shouldn't have suggested it. Today's events and the potential repercussions, already had her mind churning. Add to that the temptation of an incredibly sexy, compelling man that she'd essentially been crushing on for years and she'd probably get zero sleep.

She crossed the room to put some distance between them and sat on the sectional. "Now that you have the house in town for when you're investigating, does your team stay with you there or do they pile in here with sleeping bags?"

To her dismay, he crossed the room and sat beside her, completely scattering her focus.

"Neither. I've never brought them with me."

For a man with dark brown eyes, it was amazing how expressive they could be. Had she noticed those gold flecks before, around the iris?

"Hannah?"

"Sorry, what?"

Those expressive eyes crinkled at the corners as he smiled. "You were asking about my team. Was there something else on your mind?"

Him. And she was pretty sure he knew it. She shoved her hair back behind her ears. What had she been asking? Oh right. His team. Wait. What had he said? "Your team doesn't come to Beauchamp with you? Ever?"

"I'd hoped to bring a few of them at some point to help me. But after creating The Justice Seekers, it took far longer to recruit and build the team than I'd anticipated. Not to mention the time involved just to run the company. Later, the idea of pulling anyone off other cases to work on mine never felt right. My brother is gone. Nothing I do will bring him back. It's hard to justify diverting resources when our clients need our help."

"I understand the dilemma. But *you're* important

too. You have every right to expend resources to resolve this, especially considering it's ripped your family apart. Olivia said you almost never talk to your parents or your other sisters, Ava and Charlotte. And the only time you talk to your younger brother, Wyatt, is when he brings Olivia up to visit you."

"The others have called, or been up to visit too."

"Really? How often?"

When he hesitated, she held up her hands. "Sorry. That was way too personal. It's easy to forget that you just met me when it feels as if I've known you for a long time."

His mouth quirked in a half smile. "Olivia talks about me that much, huh?"

"You're her favorite topic."

His half smile morphed into a full-out grin. "I bet that makes Wyatt furious. Especially since she lives with him. It's probably a sore spot between them."

"You don't seem to mind."

He shrugged. "Wyatt blames me for hurting our family. He says that if I hadn't started the FBI investigation and launched the civil suit after Landon's death, then my family's friends wouldn't have turned against them. It took a long time after my parents told me to stop visiting for the community to no longer treat them like pariahs. I imagine if you'd listened to Wyatt all these years instead of Olivia, you'd probably think I'm the devil."

"Not a chance. Even if Olivia hadn't bragged on you, I've seen for myself your integrity and character. You were willing to let Murphy lock you up because you wanted to protect *me*, knowing it could cost your *life*.

Do you realize how incredible and rare that is? For a person to put others first, even if it means sacrificing themselves?" She scoffed. "I'll bet the real reason your brother resents you is because he knows he's not half the man you are. And it's your family who's hurt you, not the other way around. They've abandoned you, even though everyone knows you send them gobs of money all the time. I mean, come on, your parents' house is practically a mansion. Your mom was a teacher, like mine was. And your dad worked in some factory downtown. I can't see them affording that place on their retirement alone. Your money is good enough for them, but you're not? How hypocritical is that? As far as I'm concerned, they should be falling all over themselves begging for your forgiveness."

He stared at her so intently her face heated with embarrassment. "Oh gosh, I did it again. I overstepped. I shouldn't have said—"

Her next words were stopped by his lips against hers. The kiss was so unexpected that she barely managed to respond before it was over. But for such a short kiss, it packed an incredible punch. Her body felt incinerated from the inside out and she was tingling all over. But more than that, the aching sweetness of his touch had her heart melting. It was as if she'd felt everything he'd felt—the longing, the heat, but also the hurt and pain he'd suffered for so long. If his family, if the people who'd rejected and blamed him all these years for their own failings were here right now, she'd make it her quest to have them leave feeling ashamed for their actions. Or, better yet, she'd have them groveling at Mason's feet for the injustices they'd piled on him.

His hand shook as he gently feathered her hair back from her face, then dropped his hand to his side. "Thank you," he said, his voice raspy. "I can't remember the last time anyone defended me like that. And I didn't know how badly I needed to hear that until you said it." He let out a ragged breath, his lips curving in a wry smile. "But this shouldn't be about me. What matters is figuring out how to extricate you from this mess without destroying your future." He cleared his throat, his jaw tightening. "And we need to find Audrey's killer."

She stared at him in wonder. He was *still* more concerned about others than himself. But what surprised and dismayed her was the raw emotion in his voice when he'd said Audrey's name.

"You still care about her, don't you? After all these years, and the things she did to… I mean—dang it. Forget I went there. I don't know what's wrong with me today. I swear I'm not usually this awful." She fisted her hand on the couch, ashamed that she'd been about to say something very unflattering about a woman he'd loved, maybe still loved.

He tilted her chin up until she met his gaze. To her immeasurable relief, there was no anger, or censure in his eyes. There was only understanding, tinged with grief. "It's okay, Hannah. I'm well aware of Audrey's past. It's not exactly a secret around here that she cheated on me. And just like you believe in me, I'm getting a crash course today on believing in you too. You've got a good heart. You're only trying to look out for me. I understand that." He pressed a whisper-soft kiss against her forehead, then gently threaded his fingers through hers. "My feelings for Audrey are…complicated. I don't know that I can explain it. We basically grew up together. Her past is inextricably linked with mine. No matter what happens in the future, I imagine I'll always care about her."

She stared down at their joined hands, blinking back the tears burning in her eyes. "Hearts are complicated, aren't they? Truth be told, Johnny and I probably had more hard times than good. But through it all, we loved each other." She shook her head in wonder. "Here it is, six years later, and that love hasn't faded. The pain has, thank God, or I wouldn't be able to function." She raised her head and met his gaze. "That's what I want for you. Some kind of closure over your brother's death, and Audrey's, so your pain will fade too."

His answering smile was sad, but determined. "I hope so too. I assume Johnny was your late husband?"

She nodded. "Johnathan James Cantrell. But he always hated the name Johnathan." She smiled in remembrance. "He wouldn't even let me call him Johnathan in our wedding vows."

Mason laughed softly. "Sounds like he had strong views."

"Oh, he did. We both did. Two hardheaded people can make for a lot of fireworks. It actually helped our relationship that he was gone so often. Those were our cooling-off periods between fights. But the homecomings were amazing." She winked, delighted when he laughed in response. It was good to see the shadows finally lifting from his eyes.

"He worked on oil rigs, in the Gulf, mostly. Good pay, great benefits. Until he was killed in an accident, and I realized we didn't have nearly enough life insurance. When you're young, you think you'll live forever. We weren't prepared at all. I was a homemaker, suddenly with no income, and no real job training. I had to start over, go back to school while working part-time to make the insurance money last as long as possible. Thankfully my parents let me move in with them until I was able to get my own…oh shoot." She tugged her hand free and stood. "Parents. I told my dad I'd call as soon as we got here. And there's no telling what Murphy told him. He's probably confused and worried sick."

"It's okay. You can call your dad right now and explain what happened. I need to make a few calls myself." He got up and strode to one of the shelves of electronics. He pulled two phones out of a box, pocketed one, and brought the other to her. "It's a burner. A little more sophisticated than most. It has all the bells and whistles you're used to on a typical smart phone. But it's untraceable, for the most part."

"For the most part?"

"There's really no such thing as a phone you can't trace. But as long as your father doesn't try to trace your call and you don't call anyone else, we should be fine. I can go into the outer part of the barn so you can talk without—"

"*No.* I mean, if you don't mind waiting a few minutes, would you please stay? Dad might want to talk to you too. And honestly, I could use some backup if things get testy. I didn't get my stubbornness and hardheadedness from my mom's side of the family."

He chuckled and sat back down. "No problem."

She dialed her father's personal cell and put it on speaker.

"Chief Landry."

"Daddy, I've got you on speaker here with Mason. I'm—"

"Hannah, thank God. Where are you? No. Don't answer that. Are you okay?"

"I'm fine. We're fine. Sorry it took so long to call."

He let out a ragged breath. She could picture him raking his hands through his hair, creating a halo of short white spikes all over his head.

"Dad, something, ah, unexpected happened when we were leaving the station, so I can't come back just yet."

"*Unexpected?* Are you kidding me? Is that what you call nearly running over Captain Murphy?"

She grimaced. Mason put a reassuring hand on hers. "I'm really sorry, Dad. I didn't know what else to do. He was pointing a gun at Mason. I just…reacted. I didn't think."

"Mason should have surrendered as soon as Murphy spotted him instead of getting you pulled into this."

"You're absolutely right, sir," Mason said, before she could reply. "I should have surrendered. What kind of spin is Murphy putting on what happened?"

"Before you answer, Daddy, I want to make it clear that Mason was trying to surrender. He was about to get out of my Tucson but I took off. It was my decision and mine alone."

Mason frowned, obviously not pleased with her taking the blame.

"I'm glad to hear he was trying to do the right thing," her father said. "You should have let him. Not knowing what really happened, I told Murphy that you must have been kidnapped when you went out to get something from your car. He knows you carry a gun in your purse. I said Mason probably took it and forced you to nearly run Murphy over during the escape."

"Oh for goodness' sake, Dad. Even if he hadn't jumped out of the way, I would have swerved. He was never in danger. What a pansy."

Mason coughed. It sounded suspiciously like he was trying to hide a laugh.

"Young lady—"

"It's *true*. I wish you hadn't lied for me. I don't want more charges piled on Mason."

"I can, and should, take the heat for this," Mason interjected.

"Agreed," her father said. "This is a huge problem now. There's a BOLO out for Hannah's SUV and half the force is out searching for the two of you. I need to end this before the mayor decides to call in the state police. That's something, as a law enforcement officer, that I just can't allow to happen, knowing you haven't really been abducted. Mason needs to bring you back and surrender so we can deal with this, without making it worse."

Mason nodded his agreement.

It was her turn to frown at him. "No. Absolutely not. You and I both risked *everything* to help him escape because we knew it was the right thing to do. He's innocent. You saw the video."

"The video proves he was attacked. It doesn't prove that he didn't shoot Ms. Broussard."

Mason's mouth tightened in a firm line, obviously not happy with that statement.

"He would never hurt Audrey, Dad."

"You sure about that?"

She met Mason's gaze. "I am 100 percent positive that he didn't hurt Audrey."

He stared at her in wonder, then took her hand and pressed a kiss against her knuckles. She felt that kiss all the way to her soul.

"Okay, okay," her father said. "I'm trusting your instincts. Heck, if I didn't, I wouldn't have let you go with him in the first place. But your safety comes first. You need to get back here before some nervous Nellie stumbles over your location and pulls the trigger with you caught in the middle. I don't care if you think you have the best hiding place around. Even with just my local guys out searching, I'm confident they'll find you. Most grew up around here. They're outdoorsmen, hunters, with their own scent hounds. Tracking is what they do for fun. It scares ten years off my life just thinking about you being hunted down, knowing what could happen if someone gets spooked. I promise I'll do my best to ensure Mason's safety in jail, but you have to come back."

"I'll bring her back, sir. I have a car here. They won't be looking for that like they are her Tucson."

She frowned. "You have a car?"

"I do."

"Excellent," her father said. "We need to figure out the best way to do it, though. With so many officers out searching, even if you're in a different vehicle, they might spot you. I'd say wait until dark, since most of the searchers will have to stop their efforts until daylight. But that could be just as dangerous. Any vehicle out late at night might cause suspicion and draw attention."

"How about during the morning shift change?" Mason asked. "Most of the uniforms should be at the station, finishing up reports from the night before or preparing to go on patrol for a morning shift. You still do turnover at 0700?"

Her father laughed. "You haven't forgotten much, have you, *Chief Ford*? Yes, seven o'clock. That'll work."

"No," Hannah protested. "I refuse to let him go to jail. And he can't just drop me off at the station without someone seeing him."

"You're being stubborn, Hannah," her father accused.

"Yeah, well. Wonder who I get that from?"

A heavy sigh sounded from the phone. "I want you back, safe, without the whole state out gunning for both of you. We need a plan."

Mason shot her an apologetic look. "I have an idea."

Chapter Seven

Hannah yawned and shifted her weight on the hood of her Tucson in the dilapidated-looking barn, waiting for Mason to finish putting on his so-called movie-worthy disguise and join her. She yawned again and shook her head. Just as she'd feared, she'd gotten almost no sleep last night. But not because she was lying on the other side of the sectional craving Mason's touch. Instead, she'd been angry—at her father and Mason, but mostly at herself for agreeing to this outrageous idea.

If it worked, she'd be home free. No criminal charges for having helped Mason escape. But it meant telling more lies, which she hated. And it would do exactly what she'd been trying to avoid—make things worse for him.

The only reason she'd finally agreed was that if she didn't do this, he swore he would turn himself in.

"Still mad at me?"

She stiffened at the sound of his voice.

"Since you're not looking at me, I guess the answer is yes."

She let out a pent-up breath. "I'm not mad at you.

I'm mad at myself. Everything I did to keep you from getting into more trouble was for nothing."

"You saved my life. That's a lot more than nothing."

"It only counts as saving your life if we don't throw that away today. It's risky having you drive me into town, even with a disguise."

"I'll be fine. Because of you, I'm here this morning, alive, not locked up at the mercy of an unnamed enemy. You've given me what few people around here ever have—a second chance. I promise you that I'm not going to squander it."

Tears burned her eyes. She wiped them away before they could fall. "The BOLO is for my SUV. It should be safe for *me* to drive your car to the police station while you stay here. I'll explain that I panicked when I saw Murphy in the parking garage and—"

"They'll arrest you for aiding and abetting a fugitive. I've looked at every angle I could and truly believe this is our best option. It's the only way for you to avoid criminal charges. And don't even ask me to leave you alone at the cottage. I need to be there until you're safe and back with your dad. Otherwise, you'd be too vulnerable."

"Only because of this ridiculous plan you concocted."

He remained silent, not backing down.

She tried arguing it another way. "We're just delaying the inevitable. They'll eventually realize that I helped you."

"I agree. The truth is going to come out. I certainly have no intention of remaining a fugitive my whole life. But if we can delay the truth until I figure out who killed Audrey, and can prove it, everything changes. A reasonable District Attorney would drop all charges against me at that point, and is highly unlikely to levy charges against you or your father, since you were protecting an innocent man whose life you believed was in danger. Given the history with my brother and this town, that's a rational assumption. Especially since we already have proof that two of the current deputies are involved in my abduction. Last night you said Warren Knoll is a reasonable DA. Have you changed your mind?"

She shook her head. "No. He seems fair and honest. He works in Many, half an hour from Beauchamp, so it's not like I see him every day. But I've worked with him enough on special projects to feel that I can judge his character. And there's never been a whisper of scandal about any of his cases."

"Then there's hope this will all work out. Sticking to the plan is our best chance at a good outcome all around." He put his hand on her arm. "Are you ever going to look at me?"

She sighed and grabbed her purse before sliding off the hood. Swiping at her eyes again, she turned to face him. She jumped about a foot and let out an embarrassing squeak of surprise.

He laughed, a deep rumbling sound that was the only thing familiar about the stranger looking back at her. The bearded, gray-haired man with a slightly puffy face bore no resemblance to the dark-haired, clean-shaven, tongue-swallowingly gorgeous man she'd been hearing about for years and had finally met in person just yesterday. Even his eyes were different. Instead of warm brown, they were dark blue. And the pudgy stomach was more fitting on someone like her father than a man as buff and virile as Mason.

"You look like a grandfather who's lived a hard life in a doughnut shop."

He laughed again. "I guess that means the disguise works."

"It's *Mission: Impossible* worthy. But what about your voice? If any of the police who saw you at the station hear you speak, you'll be in trouble."

"I'm used to letting my Southern come through to cover my natural Louisiana accent whenever I visit. Seems to have worked for me so far."

The sexy Southern drawl he'd just affected had her wanting to purr and curl around him. "O…kay. Works for me." She cleared her throat. "What about your height? You can't change that. You're, what, six-two?"

"Three-ish, a tad over."

"Wow."

"Good wow or bad wow?"

"Oh, it's definitely *good*." His grin and knowing look told her he realized full well that tall men were her kryptonite. If her face got any hotter, she was going to burst into flames. "I meant *not* good. Cops are naturally suspicious. Someone might be inclined to take a closer look at you because your height makes you stand out."

He reached off to the side of the Tucson and held something up.

She frowned. "A cane? I don't—"

"It's part of my disguise, for the exact reason that you just mentioned."

Grasping the cane in his right hand, he leaned heavily on it and paced in front of her. His disjointed gait and slightly stooped posture completed the look. She doubted even his hero-worshipping baby sister would recognize him.

"Okay, okay. You obviously know what you're doing."

He winked, which had her nerves jumping for a whole other reason.

Glancing at his watch, he said, "We need to get going soon or we won't make it to the cottage around shift change. Ready?"

"Shouldn't you take off the watch? It's rather expensive looking and distinctive. You had it on at the police station."

He arched a brow. "Good catch, Ms. Crime Analyst." He took it off and shoved it in the pocket of his baggy, completely unflattering jeans.

She *really* missed the suit.

He pressed some buttons on his phone. A mechanical hum sounded. The hay bales on the left side of the barn shifted and moved. In the newly revealed opening sat an older model, charcoal gray four-door Nissan Altima. Nothing fancy or eye-catching about the sedan. Definitely not the type of vehicle that would attract attention.

He'd explained last night that he always came to the barn, first thing, on his trips. He'd exchange whatever vehicle he'd driven here, whether it was his personal Mercedes or a rental car, for the Altima. Then he'd put on his disguise and head to the cottage. If the police ever pulled him over, they'd find the car's registration matched the fake driver's license under his alias.

She rounded the car and opened the passenger door. "Hannah."

She looked over the car's roof in question.

"In order for the plan to work, you can't sit in the passenger seat. Someone might see you as they drive by the car. There are also surveillance cameras all over, both public and private. Especially in the historic district since thieves tend to prey on the large number of tourists there. The cottage is just a block off that. One of the first things the cops will do in an investigation is check for video to corroborate or disprove someone's story. That will include Christopher Johnson."

She closed the door. "Makes sense. I can sit in the back seat, or even lie down, maybe covered with a blanket. But how will I get into your house without being seen?"

"That part's easy. It's a newer build with an attached garage. I can use the remote control, drive right into the garage and close the door behind us."

"Sounds good." She opened the rear door.

He slowly shook his head.

She frowned. "What now?"

"If any of those cameras show a mounded blanket in the back seat, it could raise questions when police review the videos."

She watched with growing trepidation as he moved to the back of the car. And opened the trunk.

She blinked. "You can't be serious."

"I'm afraid it gets worse."

"Worse than me riding in the trunk of your car? What could possibly be worse?"

"Those videos have time stamps. They'll show exactly when the Altima goes into the garage. The call to 911 should happen almost immediately after that, as if I'd just found you inside."

"Okay, so?"

"With the police station so close, and everyone on high alert about you missing, there will be cops at the house in less than a minute. We won't have time to stage anything. We have to stage it now." He reached into the trunk and pulled out a nylon rope.

Chapter Eight

Hannah's face heated with shame as a crime scene tech carefully cut the nylon rope off her, putting each piece in a brown paper bag. Officer Arthur Mallory sat beside her on the couch, awkwardly patting her shoulder. Her dad had invited him to share their Christmas dinner last year because Mallory's wife was out of town on an emergency business trip and he would've been all alone. Other patrol officers and detectives she knew equally well moved through the house searching for clues about where the man who'd kidnapped her had fled.

She was looking right at him.

He was standing on the front porch, clearly visible through one of the windows, talking to the first officer who'd responded to Mason's 911 call. The same officer who'd shown her around the station her first day on the job. He was a good man: honest, trustworthy, caring. And he was no doubt thanking *Christopher Johnson* for inadvertently scaring off a wanted fugitive when he pulled into the garage. And for calling 911 on behalf of the young woman they all knew and loved at the Beauchamp Police Department.

She hung her head, squeezing her eyes shut.

"Just a couple more," Mallory assured her. "I'm sorry it's taking so long. The tech has to be careful not to cut you. And he's trying to preserve as much of the rope and potential hair and fiber evidence as possible for the state lab to examine."

Her eyes flew open. Lab? She hadn't thought about that. Then again, did it really matter? The DNA on the rope would be hers and Mason's. Which furthered the narrative about him forcing her to drive him out of the parking garage and then holding her in a vacant house until the heat died down so he could get out of town without being caught. The fact that her Tucson wouldn't appear on any videos of the area would be explained by saying he parked in woods and forced her through back yards to get here. Their cover story answered every possible question, except for one. How would they explain all male DNA in the house belonging to Mason, and none to the man who owned this house and had found her?

Would *Christopher Johnson* even have to provide a DNA sample? The whole story would fall apart if they tested him and it matched Mason. They'd know she'd lied all along. But since she told them when they got here that Mason was the one who'd tied her up, there wouldn't be any reason to ask Johnson for a sample. Would there?

It was all so confusing. What had she been thinking to agree to this outrageous plan? They were all going to jail. No, to *prison*, which was infinitely worse. Mason, her father and her. Good grief. What had she done? By convincing her father to let her help Mason in the first place, she'd doomed them all. But if she hadn't helped him, he'd be dead.

Or would he?

Mason firmly believed he'd have been murdered if he'd been put in jail. Was he wrong? Should she have let her father lock him up as he'd originally wanted? Would Mason be okay? She and her father would certainly be in a better position right now, no question.

If only she could talk to Mason again. He had a way of making the crazy make sense. He could reassure her like no one else. The only way she was going to make it through this was if she believed she'd done the right thing. But she wasn't even sure about that anymore. She shook her head in frustration.

"It's okay," Mallory soothed again. "Almost done."

She nodded her thanks when she really wanted to scream.

The front door flew open, making her start in surprise. When she saw her father standing in the opening, the tears that started flowing down her face were real. She'd never been so relieved to see him in her whole life.

He rushed to the couch and dropped to his knees in front of her. The tech snipped the last of the rope, and suddenly she was clinging to her father with his arms wrapped around her. As she cried against his shoulder, his shaking hand rubbed up and down her back. Her father was always her rock, and here he was shaking. Which just had her crying harder.

Officer Mallory spoke to him in low tones, giving him an update. She tuned them both out, drinking in the comfort of her father's arms around her. It was several minutes before she was finally able to stop crying. She had to force herself to let him go, and sit back.

He grasped her upper arms, his gaze traveling over her from head to toe. "He didn't hurt you?"

She shook her head. "No, Daddy. He didn't hurt me. I promise."

He smoothed her hair back from her face. "Thank God you're okay. The EMTs checked you out already?"

"The 911 dispatcher sent an ambulance but I turned them away. I don't need anyone prodding me or sticking me with needles when nothing's wrong."

Grasping her hand in his, he pulled her to her feet. "You need to see a doctor to be sure." He addressed Officer Mallory. "Tell the detective assigned to interview Hannah that he can question her in my office after she's checked out at the hospital."

"Dad, no. Please. I don't *need* to go to the hospital."

"Yes. You do. And I'm taking you."

Her shoulders slumped in defeat.

Mallory cleared his throat. "My apologies, Chief. I should have insisted that she be examined."

"It's okay. I know how stubborn she can be."

"Dad—"

"Come on." He pulled her toward the door. As they stepped onto the porch, she risked a quick glance at Mason. But he didn't even look her way.

A chorus of cheers had her stumbling to a surprised halt. Her cheeks heated with embarrassment as about a dozen police officers in the front yard clapped and smiled, elated that the analyst they'd been working with for the past year had been safely "rescued."

She was totally going to hell for this.

Her father ushered her through the crowd toward his police-issued SUV. Once inside, she collapsed back against the seat and closed her eyes. She was such a fraud. When the truth eventually came out, they'd all hate her. And she couldn't blame them.

The SUV rumbled as it pulled away from the curb.

"I know this is tough," her father said. "But it's going to be okay. We'll get through this. Together."

She let out a deep breath and opened her eyes. Then she straightened. "Dad? This isn't the way to the police station. Please tell me you're not *actually* driving me to Sabine Medical Center. Many's half an hour away and there's no telling what kinds of tests and scans they'll insist on doing. I just want to get my interview over with and go home."

"I'm not taking you to Sabine Medical Center."

She relaxed against the seat. "Thank goodness."

"I'm taking you to Beauchamp Clinic."

"Dad."

"Consider the clinic a compromise. But we *are* going and you *will* be seen by a doctor. We're doing this by the book so it looks legit. If someone thinks it's not, you could be arrested for a felony. You get that, right? It won't matter that I'm the police chief. We have to convince people like Captain Murphy to believe you. If we don't, you and I will both be in serious trouble."

The reminder about the danger to him quelled any

further complaints. "I'm sorry about all of this. I never meant for things to get so out of control."

He reached across the middle console and patted her hand. "I knew the risks when I took those handcuffs off him instead of taking him to lockup. After seeing that video, there really wasn't any choice. I couldn't stand by and simply hope that none of my other deputies were as rotten as Abrams and Donnelly. If that decision comes back to bite me, so be it. But you're not to blame for this situation. The blame lies squarely on whoever killed Ms. Broussard and framed an innocent man."

Tears threatened yet again. She breathed through it, holding them back. She'd never been a crier, but no one would believe that if they'd seen her yesterday, or today. Next to losing her husband, this was the roughest thing, emotionally, that she'd ever faced. Apparently she wasn't as tough as she thought.

Her father steered around some potholes, bumping through one of the town's worst intersections. "I didn't see Mason at the cottage. I thought he was going to pose as the homeowner and supposedly discover you so you wouldn't be vulnerable and tied up while he went somewhere else to call 911. Did he change his mind? Leave you alone? If he did, so help me, I'll—"

"Seriously? Dad, he was on the front porch talking to one of your officers. You didn't see him?"

He gave her a surprised look. "The guy with the beard? And the cane?"

"Yes."

"I remember glancing at him as I nodded at Jennings.

Nothing sparked any recognition. Guess he was right about that disguise of his."

"And?"

He rolled his eyes. "And he didn't abandon you. I shouldn't have jumped to that conclusion. Okay?"

"Okay. And you're right, that was an incredible disguise. I doubt his own mother would recognize him." She wrinkled her nose. "Not that she visits him enough to even remember what he looks like. I've probably seen him more these past few days than she has in the past eight years."

His brows arched. "I take it he's not close to his family?"

"The other way around. It was their choice. I kind of hate them for turning their backs on him."

"*Hate*'s a strong word, Hannah Rose."

She smiled. "I know I'm in trouble if you're using my middle name. Usually Mom's the one who calls me Hannah Rose."

He shot her a pained look. "Speaking of mothers, *yours* is worried sick about you. I called her when I got official word that you'd been found safe. But she'll still need to see you for herself. So will your sisters."

"You told them I was kidnapped?"

"Honey, I didn't *have* to tell them. It's all over the news. They called me in a panic last night. Mary drove in from New Orleans around midnight. Sarah got here an hour ago from Baton Rouge. Their husbands stayed home with their kids and dogs. I hated lying to them, especially your mom, but I had to. We need everyone to act the way they would if you'd really been abducted. It's a lot easier if they don't have to pretend."

She groaned. "This hole we're digging is getting deeper and deeper."

"I know. I'm trying to figure a way out of it. It all hinges on finding out the truth about Ms. Broussard's murder. At my request, Detective Latimer is heading up a large team of detectives on this case. It's their top priority."

He turned down the side street that led to the clinic. "Will you stay at our house for a few days? It would make your mother calm down after such a scare."

"I'll come for a quick visit. But please don't try to guilt me into staying with you and Mom longer than that. I need some normalcy in my life after this roller coaster we've been on. Besides, Sarah and Mary will be in the spare rooms. You don't need me piling on your couch. And, honestly, if I have to endure a couple of days of questions from them, I'll probably cave. I'll be lucky if I can hold it together long enough to survive the questioning at the station later and not spill the beans to Mom and them."

"I get it. I do. If your mom tries to force the issue, I'll take your side, try to help her understand that you need your space." He crossed through another intersection. "We're just a few blocks from the clinic. I promised to give that Bishop guy an update about the search for Mason this morning. This seems as good a time as any." He nodded toward his personal cell phone sitting in the console. "Would you mind pressing the first contact under favorites? You can put it on speaker mode."

Moments later, Mason's employee answered the call. "Bishop."

"Bishop, this is police chief Mitch Landry in Beauchamp, Louisiana, calling to give you that update I promised."

"Mason got away safely. The kidnapping ruse worked and you're taking your daughter to the hospital to be checked out."

Her father frowned. "Your boss was talking to one of my patrol officers last I saw. No way did he have a chance to call you. How do you know all of that?"

"It's my job to know."

He rolled his eyes. "Let me guess. Mason has one of those fancy, hidden alarm systems at the cottage, transmitting to you?"

When Bishop didn't say anything, her father swore softly. "It's *my* job to keep my daughter safe," he snapped. "Mason didn't tell me he was letting you in on the truth about this kidnapping farce. I don't want anything getting out and hurting Hannah."

"I understand your concerns. But you can't expect us to trust your legal system, not given what's happened in the past. We're going on the offensive and will do whatever it takes to get justice for Mason. Beauchamp, Louisiana, is about to become really uncomfortable for a lot of people."

Her father's jaw worked. Hannah didn't think she'd ever seen him this angry. "Be warned, Bishop. I'll fight for justice too, because it's the right thing to do. But protecting my daughter comes first. Are we clear?"

"Crystal, sir."

"But you're not going to promise that she won't get hurt in this fight of yours, are you?"

"I don't think either of us can promise that."

Hannah put her hand on his shoulder to stop whatever he was about to say. Listening to Mason's employee sounding so calm and in control, somehow had a settling effect on her. She'd never met this Bishop guy, but his confidence was comforting. More importantly, Mason trusted him. That went a long way with her. And knowing that she and her father weren't in this fight alone was a huge relief.

"It's okay, Dad. Like you said earlier, we both knew we could get in serious trouble when we helped Mason escape. All we can do now is keep trying to protect him, and each other, and hope for the best."

He turned into the Beauchamp Clinic parking lot. "All right, Bishop. We're all going to do what we feel we have to do. When can I expect my town to be invaded by these Justice Seekers?"

"We're already here."

Chapter Nine

Being poked and prodded at the clinic had been a demoralizing experience, especially since it was unnecessary. But Hannah would go back for more torture if she could avoid what was next: an interrogation by one of Beauchamp PD's finest.

She clutched her father's hand as the police station's first floor elevator doors closed. He pressed the button for the second floor.

"It'll be okay, Hannah. Even if things don't go the way we hope they will, neither of us has a criminal record. The DA would take that into account when considering whether or not to press charges."

Neither of them acknowledged what he hadn't said, that even if they both avoided prison time, both of their careers would be over if they were convicted of a crime.

The elevator dinged and she let go of his hand. She drew a bracing breath just as the doors opened, and another painful gauntlet began. In spite of shift change being long past, the squad room was full. Officers who should have been on patrol hurried to greet her, hug her, tell her how they'd prayed for her safe return.

Her father helped as best he could, steering her toward his office—which sported a brand-new door and frame to replace the ones that Al had busted. She was about ten feet from sanctuary when a familiar face a few desks away had her stopping so fast that her father ran into her.

"Hannah, goodness, what…" He went silent when he saw what she saw, or rather, *who* she saw.

Mason Ford.

Except that he was Christopher Johnson to the detective talking to him. His cane rested against the desk and he seemed completely at ease, gesturing with his hands as he answered whatever question was being asked.

Hannah spotted Al standing a few desks away, talking to some patrol officers. Two more deputies who'd worked here when Mason was the chief of police were in the squad room too. What was he thinking, risking his life like this? What if one of them realized who he was?

"Ms. Cantrell? Is that you?"

She jerked her head toward Mason.

He grinned and rose from his chair and leaned on his cane. "Good to see you looking so well."

Her father put his arm around her shoulders, which was probably the only reason she didn't fall down. She cleared her throat. "Um, Mr.—I'm so sorry. I forgot your name."

He gave her a grandfatherly smile. "After what you went through, I wouldn't expect you to remember. It's Johnson. Christopher Johnson."

"Mr. Johnson, thank you again for…rescuing me. I'm in your debt."

"Wasn't nothin'. All I did was walk into my living room and call 911. Glad I could help."

Her father, perhaps because so many people were turning to watch, stepped forward and offered his hand. "I didn't get a chance to thank you at the cottage. I'm Chief Landry, Hannah's father. Thank you for helping her."

Mason switched hands on his cane, wobbling as he shook her father's hand. "Glad I was there."

Al noticed the exchange and hurried over. "How about you finish up that statement, Mr. Johnson. I need to talk to the chief."

"Sure, sure. That's fine." He eased down into the chair, grimacing as if his arthritis was acting up.

Hannah couldn't believe how comfortable he seemed in a room full of people dedicated to throwing him in jail.

"Come on, Hannah," her father urged, steering her toward his office again.

A moment later the three of them were cocooned inside. She gratefully took one of the seats in front of her father's desk while he sat behind it.

Al surprised her by sitting in one of the other guest chairs. "Are you feeling up to answering some questions, Hannah? Did the doctors say you're okay?"

She glanced at her father before looking back at Al. "You're the one who's going to interrogate me?"

He smiled. "No, ma'am. An *interview* is reserved for suspects. You're the victim in this. I'd like to have a conversation with you, ask some questions to make sure I have all the facts right. Your father can stay, unless you don't want him here."

"Oh no, he can stay. I'd like that."

"Good, good. This shouldn't take long. But if you're not feeling well or ready—"

"Oh, I'm ready." She smiled. "I'm glad it's you who's questioning me. A familiar, friendly face will make this much easier."

"Glad to hear it." He pulled a small electronic device from his shirt pocket. "I'm going to record our conversation. Is that okay?"

Her smile dimmed. "Um, sure."

He pressed some buttons, then set the recorder on the arm of his chair. "For the record, this is Detective Harvey Latimer questioning Ms. Hannah Cantrell in the matter of her alleged kidnapping by Mason Ford."

She winced at his "alleged" remark, but understood it had to do with Mason being presumed innocent until proven guilty.

After stating the date and time for the recording, he rested his massive forearms on his knees, making her feel crowded and a little uneasy. His earlier smile seemed like a distant memory. It had been replaced with a hard look that was all business.

"Now, then, Hannah. Let's start with the incident in the parking garage, where you almost ran over Captain Murphy."

Ten minutes later, she was squeezing the arms of her chair so hard she was amazed they hadn't broken. If this was supposed to be a *conversation*, she couldn't imagine what an interview would be like. It had her wondering if he'd seen through her lies and was trying to make her crack. But her father didn't seem concerned. Maybe these were softball questions after all. But it sure didn't feel that way.

A knock on the door had Al frowning. But Hannah was pathetically grateful for the reprieve. Her father called out and the door opened to reveal Officer Mallory. He smiled when he saw Hannah, then addressed her father.

"Chief." He motioned toward the squad room. "There are some people here to see you."

"We're a little busy right now."

"Sorry for interrupting. But I felt you'd want to know about this. The leader, I guess you could call him, is adamant about talking to you, immediately."

"Leader?"

"Some guy who calls himself Bishop. I don't know if that's his first or last name. Apparently he works for a group called The Justice Seekers."

Her father's face was carefully blank. "Justice what?"

She realized the only way they could both know about the Seekers was if they'd heard it from Mason. Thank goodness her dad had thought of that.

Mallory leaned against the doorframe. "Seekers. They said that's the name of a company Mason Ford created. Apparently they investigate crimes and protect people, or something like that. Most of them are former law enforcement or ex-military. They're demanding to speak to you."

Her father swore and seemed genuinely aggravated. She knew he hadn't been looking forward to Bishop and the rest of Mason's team showing up, so he probably wasn't acting. Then again, maybe he was. Police lied to suspects all the time. Maybe extending that to other things wasn't a stretch. The realization that her father was a good liar wasn't comforting. And it had her wondering whether every officer and detective she knew was just as skilled.

No wonder so many police who'd worked for Mason years ago had been corrupt without him realizing it. It also helped explain how her father's two deputies concealed their own corruption. Who else around here was in on what had happened to Mason? And how could she trust any of these people in the future? Then again, how could they trust her?

She sighed and tuned back in to what her father was saying, something about putting the visitors in a conference room.

"Chief, we don't *have* a conference room big enough to hold all of them."

"*All* of them? How many are there?"

"Well, if I counted right, there are at least a dozen of the Justice Seekers and—"

"A dozen?"

Mallory nodded.

Hannah exchanged a surprised glance with Al. Both of them leaned to the side to look at the squad room through the open doorway. She was stunned to see so many men and women milling around that she didn't know. Some of the men were as tall as Mason. One of them wore a black Stetson. Another stood slightly apart from the others, leaning against a wall, his expression unreadable. She instinctively pegged him as Bishop and wondered if she was right.

Her father tapped his hand on his desk as he considered the problem. "We can fit a dozen people in the clerk of courts conference room on the first floor. Al's lead detective on the case, so he needs to be at the meeting too. It'll be tight. But I suppose a couple of those so-called Seekers can stand if need be."

Mallory cleared his throat. "The, ah, Justice Seekers aren't the only ones here to see you. They brought some other people with them."

"Other people? Who?"

"Mr. Ford's lawyer. Actually he has two of them—one from Tennessee and another from right here in Louisiana. I guess she's his *official* lawyer because she's licensed to practice law in this state while the other lawyer isn't. There's also a homicide detective from Gatlinburg. One of our own judges, the District Attorney—"

"Wait. Warren Knoll is here, and a judge?"

Mallory tugged at his collar. "That's not the worst of it, Chief."

Her father gave him an impatient look. "Then what *is* the worst, Mallory?"

There was a commotion in the doorway behind him. He moved back and another man stepped into the opening, his dark suit and tie in stark contrast to his crisp white shirt.

"I think he means me." He pulled his credentials from one of his suit pockets and held them up. "Jaylen Holland, special agent with the FBI."

Chapter Ten

From his seat in the squad room, Mason observed the chaos erupting around him. The detective he'd been talking to was now arguing with Dalton. Another was backing away from former FBI profiler, Bryson Anton, who was adamantly arguing that any imbecile could see that Mason wasn't a murderer. Even Bishop hadn't escaped the mayhem. Patrol officers were buzzing around him like angry gnats, demanding information about the Seekers. In response, Bishop was being Bishop. He ignored them, focusing instead on the open doorway to the chief's office.

Not the kind of reception Mason had hoped for. Emotions were running high, which had people choosing sides rather than realizing they were fighting for the same thing—truth and justice. And yet, in spite of the chaos, progress *was* being made. That shouldn't have surprised him, since he'd put Bishop in charge. He just wished that he could have warned Hannah about the newest development. He'd only found out about it himself while texting Bishop from the men's room down the hall.

Bishop had assembled the Seekers and a few others and met with District Attorney Knoll this morning. It went relatively well, but the DA had surprised everyone by immediately assembling his own team and heading to Beauchamp PD. The boulder was rolling down hill and picking up speed. All Mason could do was prepare for damage control—and hope the damage wasn't catastrophic.

Bishop straightened, a signal to Mason that the chief was about to emerge from his office. He stepped out, followed by FBI Special Agent Holland, who'd worked with the Seekers many times in the past. Behind him were Al and Hannah. She looked pale and worried. Mason wished he could reassure her.

Al charged off toward his fellow detectives and officers, rounding them up and ushering some to grab chairs while sending others to the elevator. After a brief exchange with the chief, Dalton and Bryson led the Seekers in helping the detectives move desks to the side and form a circle of chairs in the middle of the squad room. Mason hobbled out of the way, careful to lean on his cane in keeping with his disguise.

"Ladies and gentlemen," the chief called out above the noise. "If you're one of the detectives investigating the Broussard murder, please stay. Likewise, if you're a Seeker or one of their guests, please stick around. Everyone else, take an early lunch or head out on patrol. As soon as the room's available again, I'll have a department text sent out to let you know."

Muted grumbling met his announcement. But those

not invited to stay began heading toward the elevators or stairs while others moved toward the circle of chairs.

The chief seemed surprised to see *Christopher Johnson* still there. He motioned to one of the departing patrol officers. "Escort Mr. Johnson to the break room and tag one of the detectives to finish his interview in there."

Mason tapped his finger on the desk, twice, to signal Bishop. No way in hell was he missing this. His future—and possibly Hannah's—was on the line.

"We want Mr. Johnson in the meeting," Bishop called out. "We might have questions for him."

The chief frowned. "I don't think that's a good idea. He's a civilian—"

"So are we. This isn't business as usual. And we have a limited amount of time before our Gatlinburg guests have to leave. If we need to call Mr. Johnson back later, it will delay things."

"I still don't think—"

"Let him stay." Knoll, who'd been quietly observing the chaos, stepped forward. "I'm all for saving time. Today's events have already wrecked my schedule. I'm sure I'm not the only one."

Before the chief could protest again, Mason headed to the circle of chairs.

Hannah hesitated. "Dad, should I go home?"

He dug in his pants pocket for his keys and handed them to her. "Take my SUV. I'll call you when this is over so you can pick me up."

She took the keys and started toward the elevator.

"Wait a minute." Knoll motioned to her. "I'd like

Ms. Cantrell to stay. She has far more to add than Mr. Johnson. Let's all sit down, shall we?"

Her eyes widened with concern, but she followed her father and sat beside him.

Mason would have given anything to hold her hand right now. As if thinking the same thing, her father squeezed her hand, smiling encouragingly. But when the DA took the seat on the other side of the chief, his smile faded.

Chief Landry glanced around the room. "I guess I should get us started. I'm not really sure what—"

"No worries. I've got this." Knoll smiled, but there was no amusement in it. "I'll get things rolling. If you don't mind, of course."

"Um, sure. Please. Go ahead." The worry lines on Landry's forehead deepened.

"Excellent. All of the people in this room have a connection to the ongoing murder investigation of Audrey Broussard, or the suspect, Mason Ford. On behalf of those who don't know everyone in the room, and as a reminder for those of us who've only recently met, I'll make some introductions."

He shifted in his chair, as if settling in for the long haul. "I'm Warren Knoll, District Attorney over the 11th Judicial District, which basically means all of Sabine Parish. To my right is the honorable Judge Richard Guidry. To my left is police chief Mitch Landry, then his daughter, Hannah Cantrell, who's also a crime data analyst for Beauchamp PD. I see esteemed defense attorney Bernette Armstrong over there." He smiled. "We've been on opposite sides of a courtroom more times than I can count but are still cordial, so that's saying something. To her left is Jaylen Holland, special agent with the FBI. I believe you're from the Knoxville office?"

Jaylen nodded. "I've got special permission from the local field office to advise on the case involving the abduction of Mr. Ford. The FBI's interest is because he was taken across state lines. Also, based on some of the evidence, we might have another corruption case brewing against Beauchamp PD. I'll want to interview deputies Abrams and Donnelly in the very near future."

"Yes, yes. We'll see that you meet with the illustrious deputies in good time. Let's see, Mr. LeMarcus Johnson—can we call you LeMarcus to distinguish you from the other Mr. Johnson in the room, who's a witness in this case?"

"Of course."

"I believe you're Mr. Ford's personal attorney, with assistance from Mrs. Armstrong since you're not licensed in our state. Is that correct?"

"It is, sir. I'm also employed as one of the Justice Seekers."

"Right, I'd forgotten that. Bishop, you're the leader of the Seekers—"

"No, sir. Mason Ford's our leader. But I'm heading up our current case."

"My apologies for not making that distinction."

"What are Justice Seekers?" Al asked.

Knoll motioned to Bishop. "I'll let you take that."

Bishop sighed, as if he was tired of answering that

question, which Mason imagined he was. Few people around here had likely ever heard of his company.

After Bishop's explanation, Knoll said, "To save time, Bishop, can we skip introducing the rest of your team unless they speak during the meeting?"

"Yes, sir. I would, however, like to mention that seated two chairs to my right is Detective Erin Sampson, from Gatlinburg PD."

"Very good," Knoll said. "From our side, we have a large team of detectives working this case. The lead detective is Harvey Latimer. Most of us know him as Al, for reasons I've honestly forgotten. Something to do with Twinkies, I believe."

Al grinned and raised his hand in greeting to everyone. "Yippee-ki-yay, folks."

Mason couldn't help smiling at the *Die Hard* movie reference.

Chief Landry motioned toward one of the people Knoll hadn't mentioned. "Captain Murphy, I don't believe you're working this case. You can go."

"He's my guest," Knoll said. "He stays."

Landry's mouth tightened. Mason imagined he was fuming inside, being treated so casually when this was his police department. The DA should have met with the chief privately first. The fact that he hadn't revealed an alarming lack of respect. And yet, Knoll had seemed fair and reasonable in his meeting with Bishop, according to Bishop's texts. But for some reason he wasn't extending that same courtesy to the chief. That had Mason concerned that the DA might know more than either Mason or Bishop had thought.

Knoll crossed his legs at the ankle. "Let's get started. When I arrived at my office this morning, Bishop and a lot of the people in this room *demanded* to speak to me. They proceeded to show me some compelling videos and launched a long list of complaints against Beauchamp PD, my office and pretty much anyone in law enforcement in the state of Louisiana. I was then threatened with a lawsuit that would drain Sabine Parish's coffers back to the Stone Age if I didn't immediately intervene in the miscarriage of justice going on here in Beauchamp. I've left out some of the more colorful language that was used." He arched a brow. "Bishop, did I summarize that accurately?"

Bishop gave him a reluctant smile. "Close enough."

Knoll glanced around the room. "One of the many *interesting* topics we discussed was presented by Special Agent Holland. Since the FBI has interceded here before, he was well versed in this town's rather sordid past regarding the appalling handling of the Mandy DuBois/Landon Ford case, which he proceeded to remind me about—not that I needed the reminder. The case is notorious around here even though I wasn't the DA at that time. Near the end of the meeting, my office was informed that Ms. Cantrell had just been rescued after allegedly having been abducted yesterday by Mr. Ford. Knowing her father, Chief Landry, would want to be with her, I asked Captain Murphy to fill me in on some of the details of the past few days. It was quite enlightening."

Landry exchanged a concerned glance with Hannah before looking at Knoll again.

The DA continued. "I think everyone here is well aware of the alleged abduction of Mr. Ford in Gatlinburg. And Gatlinburg Detective Sampson has already made her outrage painfully clear to me about Mr. Ford's subsequent treatment here in Beauchamp."

"Don't forget," she said, "that I also brought a warrant for Abrams and Donnelly, and an extradition request."

"I haven't forgotten. But my main goal at the moment is to keep my parish from becoming embroiled in yet another expensive lawsuit. And more importantly, ensuring that innocent people aren't hurt, as they have been in the past under the leadership of a previous mayor and an embarrassingly large number of corrupt public officials, even former deputies within this police department."

The chief was frowning again, his gaze fixed on Knoll.

"In regards to Mr. Ford and what occurred in Gatlinburg, videos prove without question that he was viciously attacked, drugged, abducted and transported across state lines. There's also zero doubt in my mind that two of the men involved in those crimes are deputies of Beauchamp PD. They have, rightfully so, been placed under arrest. It's my recommendation they be fired immediately. My office will assist Detective Sampson with extradition proceedings. Chief Landry? Any issues with that?"

He shook his head. "None."

"Do the lawyers present have anything further to say on that particular topic?"

LeMarcus and Armstrong both shook their heads.

"Moving on, I've got a few things to say regarding the tragedy of Ms. Broussard's murder. We will of course do everything in our power to fully, and lawfully, investigate what happened. And I personally guarantee that none of the shenanigans that happened in the DuBois/Ford case years ago will happen again. Evidence will *not* be tampered with, fabricated, or disappear on my watch. Bishop, your team will be given unprecedented access to work alongside our detectives on the case. I understand your goal is to prove your boss innocent. Our goal is to find out who murdered Ms. Broussard. If your faith in Mr. Ford is justified, I don't see any reason those goals should conflict with one another."

Bishop's brows raised. "No, sir. They shouldn't."

Knoll looked at Detective Latimer. "Al, you'll get a copy of the videos from Gatlinburg that I mentioned. In one of them, you'll see a black Ford Expedition. The Seekers had an expert enhance footage taken in downtown Gatlinburg that same day. While I don't understand how this particular puzzle piece fits with everything else, there's no question that the SUV was registered to Ms. Broussard, and that she's the one who drove Abrams, Donnelly and three as yet unidentified masked men to Mr. Ford's home, where they proceeded with the aforementioned assault and abduction of Mr. Ford."

Al's eyes widened in surprise. Either he hadn't heard about the SUV, or no one had told him the theory yet that Audrey might somehow be involved.

"Another thing to consider in your investigation, Al,

is the video of the assault. It clearly shows Mr. Ford's pistol was taken from him by Abrams. And yet, that same pistol is miraculously in Ms. Broussard's home when Mr. Ford awakens from his drug-induced state. If the ballistics come back proving Mr. Ford's gun killed her, that's extremely suspicious. Given all of the other circumstances leading up to him being in Ms. Broussard's home—including her history of contentious visits to Gatlinburg, as relayed to me by the Justice Seekers— I'm inclined to have more than reasonable doubts that Mr. Ford is the one who pulled the trigger. I strongly encourage you to look at both of our jailed deputies as suspects in the murder."

Stunned didn't come close to describing how Mason felt right now. From what Bishop had told him, Mason had been expecting a fair shake. But he hadn't expected the DA to essentially declare Mason not guilty.

Al straightened. "Sir, while I admire and respect Chief Ford from when I worked for him, I'm not prepared to say he didn't do this. The investigation is just starting. And you have to consider his most recent actions when judging his character. He kidnapped Ms. Cantrell."

"I'm not asking you to stop your investigation. What I'm telling you is that the bar is extremely high on this one. In order for my office to take this to court, you'll have to show me solid evidence, untainted by Abrams's and Donnelly's actions, that definitively proves guilt."

Al crossed his arms. "Understood."

"As to your comment about him kidnapping Ms. Cantrell, I've got a few thoughts to share on that."

Mason's stomach sank. This was the part he'd wished he could warn Hannah about. As if realizing he was looking at her, she glanced his way, her eyes wide with uncertainty. But he couldn't even nod his head without risking giving himself away. It was torture sitting there and doing nothing.

Knoll turned to face Landry. "Chief, when exactly were you going to tell me about the hidden hallway behind the wall in your office?"

Her father's face reddened. Mason exchanged a surprised glance with Bishop. The DA hadn't mentioned the secret entrance in the earlier meeting. Bishop had assumed he'd bought the theory that Mason had climbed out the window. Now the DA's poor treatment of the chief began to make sense.

Knoll leaned slightly forward to look at Hannah on the other side of her father. "You and I have discussed the history of this town. I know you studied it in school, as did I. It shouldn't come as a surprise that I also know a lot of these buildings have hidden panels off the stairways that access secret hallways. Just like the one that leads into your father's office."

Her father stiffened. "Now, wait a minute—"

"You might also be interested to know, Hannah, that our security guys sent me footage from the cameras in the parking garage. I'll bet you didn't think about the cameras when you and Mason exited the back stairs and got into your SUV, did you?"

The chief slumped like a balloon losing air.

Hannah tilted her chin defiantly as she addressed Knoll. "No, actually. It never occurred to me."

He laughed, seemingly amused. "The cameras also recorded you nearly running over Captain Murphy."

"I was in control of my vehicle at all times. If he hadn't moved, I would have swerved. He wasn't in any real danger."

A gasp across the room had her looking at Murphy.

"Oh, come on, Paul." She rolled her eyes. "How often did you and I drag race in high school? I whipped your butt every time and never crashed. And you know I'd never hurt you, or anyone else. You *know* it."

His face reddened. A few of the people in the room chuckled. "All right. In hindsight, maybe I made too big a deal out of it. But you can't deny you were helping a fugitive escape."

"No, I can't and won't deny it. And I'd do it again if given the chance."

"Hannah," her father cautioned.

She shook her head. "No, I've been silent too long."

"Ms. Cantrell." This time it was LeMarcus who spoke up. "As a lawyer, I strongly urge you not to say anything else without your own attorney present."

"I appreciate the advice," she said. "But I'm not taking it." She leaned forward to look at Knoll. "Enough of these games. You obviously know that I helped Mason escape. What you don't know is that as soon as Captain Murphy saw us, Mason wanted to surrender so he could keep me from getting into trouble. I'm the one who refused to stop. Why? Because I had every reason to fear for Mr. Ford's life. You mentioned this town's tarnished past. Mason's brother was railroaded to prison in a setup like the one playing out against Mason. Landon paid for the corruption with his life. I wasn't about to let that happen to Mason, not if there was anything I could do to stop it. Go ahead, arrest me if you want. But I won't apologize for doing the right thing."

Knoll's eyebrows had arched so high they were practically at his hairline by the time she finished. "Is there anything else you want to add to that speech?"

She leaned forward again. "As a matter of fact, there is. Mr. Ford never pulled a gun on me. He didn't kidnap me. Instead, he risked his own life by putting me in that cottage so I could go home to my family. He did that because he was worried that a search party might shoot me by accident. What you see here, Mr. Knoll, is a pattern. Every time someone needs help or protection, Mason Ford's first reaction is to help them, no matter the cost to himself." She turned her head and glared at Al. "*That* is the measure of his character. How dare you impugn him by suggesting otherwise. Your time would be better spent doing your job—finding out who killed Audrey and dropping all charges against the innocent man who has only ever loved her, even when she didn't deserve that love. He is the absolute last person who would harm her." She crossed her arms and sat back. "Now I'm done."

Mason, along with everyone else in the room, stared at her in shock. His heart had seemed to crack a little with every fierce declaration she'd made, every argument she'd said in his defense. He'd been agonizing about how she'd handle the revelation about the parking garage cameras, which was the information Bishop had told him right before the meeting. But in his worst-case imagined scenario, he'd never expected her to admit to everything, leaving herself completely vulnerable to prosecution.

He had to do something. He couldn't sit here hiding behind a disguise while this incredible, strong, amazing woman was going to battle for him, and putting herself at risk. He jumped up from his chair, only to be pushed back down by Bishop. Mason hadn't even seen him coming toward him.

"Oh, so sorry. Mr. Johnson, was it? I didn't realize you were getting up too. Were you heading to that coffee bar over there like me?"

Mason narrowed his eyes in warning.

Bishop narrowed his eyes too. He wasn't backing down. "Come on, I'll help you." He pulled Mason to his feet and shoved his cane in his hand.

It was either go along with Bishop's ploy, or deck him. While Mason debated his choices, Dalton was suddenly on his other side.

"Feeling a little shaky, Mr. Johnson? Here, we'll both help you." They each grabbed an arm, and even though he was just as big as either of them, together they were a force to be reckoned with.

When they were all three in the alcove, Mason jerked his arms free. He glared at them. Dalton grinned. Bishop busied himself making three cups of coffee. Mason leaned past the edge of the wall, frowning when Dalton blocked his way.

"I'm just going to see what they're doing," Mason gritted out in a harsh whisper.

Dalton moved, but not enough for Mason to easily

get past him. He shook his head in exasperation, and peered around him to see what was going on.

Knoll shifted in his chair. "I think I've got the information I needed to make some decisions. I'll start with Mr. Ford. The kidnapping charge will be dropped. However, the murder charge stands."

Once again, the room erupted in chaos, with nearly everyone talking at once. Mason let out a deep breath, while Dalton swore beside him.

Knoll held up his hands, motioning for everyone to be quiet. When they settled down, he said, "I'm not saying he's guilty. But I can't ignore that he was found holding a gun over a murdered woman's body. Al will continue his investigation and once he's done, I'll make the final decision on whether to proceed with prosecution or drop all charges. However, I'm going to do something I've never done before in a murder case. I'm recommending that Mr. Ford be released on bail."

Mason blinked, waiting for the catch.

Knoll turned to the judge, sitting on his right. "I've been assured by Bishop that Mr. Ford has the means to have left the country if he'd wanted to. Therefore, as bizarre as it seems to say this after the earlier escape, I don't consider him a flight risk. Instead of fleeing Louisiana when he easily could have, he stayed here in the parish, presumably to prove his innocence."

The judge nodded his agreement. "You and I discussed this before we came here and my opinion hasn't changed. However, out of respect for Ms. Broussard's family, the amount has to be high, commensurate with the crime."

Mrs. Armstrong called out, "How high?"

"One million dollars."

Hannah visibly recoiled in her seat and shot Mason a worried glance.

He winked.

Her eyes widened.

The two lawyers conferred for a moment, then Armstrong spoke. "Agreed. I'll have a commercial bail bond arranged as soon as this meeting is over, with the usual required percentage paid in cash so that my client can be free until trial. Or until the charges are dropped."

Knoll arched a brow. "Your client can pay one hundred and twenty thousand dollars, cash, right away?"

It was LeMarcus's turn to reply. "*Our* client can pay the entire million in cash if he has to. But obviously we prefer a bond." He pulled a sheaf of papers out of his suit jacket pocket and handed them to the other lawyer.

Armstrong glanced through the papers, then took them to Knoll. "That's Mr. Ford's current bank statement. As you can see, the required 12 percent won't be a problem. I request that the court accepts that the client will pay and grants freedom immediately."

"That's pretty brazen." Knoll shrugged. "Judge?"

He considered it a moment. "Mrs. Armstrong, do I have your word that it will be paid? Right after this meeting? Knowing you could be disbarred for lying to the court?"

"You have my word."

"Very well. The court accepts those terms. Consider Mr. Mason Ford officially free on bond. But he'll have to show up in person, to prove he hasn't fled the country, and to give me confidence he'll be here for any required court appearances."

"Agreed."

Mason exchanged glances with Bishop and Dalton, and tapped his face. They nodded in understanding and formed a human wall in front of him, casually holding their coffee cups and effectively blocking anyone from seeing him.

"Next up," Knoll said, "my decision about Ms. Cantrell."

Mason couldn't see what was going on, but he listened intently as he pulled the fake paunch out from under his shirt.

"Hannah," Knoll said, his voice taking on more of a friendly tone. "We've worked together enough that I feel confident you're telling the truth. You strongly believe in Mr. Ford's innocence, and that his life could have been forfeit if you hadn't intervened. Therefore, I'll overlook your involvement in his escape, *and* the fake kidnapping. No charges will be filed against you."

Mason smiled and worked at a piece of glue on his neck, wishing he could see her. She'd probably been too overcome with emotion since she didn't say anything. His own relief was immeasurable. Maybe Bishop and Dalton had been right to intervene when they had. Otherwise, the outcome might not have been this favorable for either him or Hannah.

"As to you, Chief," Knoll said, "that video in the garage showed more than two people in the stairwell. You were there too. Except you went through the door to the lobby instead of into the parking garage. Obviously, you had the same concerns as your daughter. However, she's a civilian and you're a trusted member of law enforcement who deliberately helped a prisoner escape and then covered it up. If you had concerns, you should have followed the chain of command by contacting both the mayor and me. Together, we would have ensured his safety and avoided this huge hullaballoo about an alleged kidnapping. *You're fired.*"

"No," Hannah cried out. "You can't do that."

"Technically, you're correct. Only the mayor can fire your father. I spoke to him on the way here and he's in full agreement. He's in the process of sending over the signed paperwork and initiating an immediate search for a new chief. In the meantime, he's already appointed an acting chief, Captain Murphy. I swore him in over the phone."

Mason clutched the counter, guilt riding him hard. He'd created The Justice Seekers to help others who'd had their law enforcement careers destroyed. And here he was, destroying Landry's career. How could Landry, or Hannah, ever forgive him? Hell, how would he forgive himself?

The sound of footsteps crossing the room had Mason lifting his head. Dalton whispered, "Landry's giving his golden eagle lapel pins, badge and gun to Murphy."

"Chief, I didn't ask for this." Murphy's voice was laced with misery. "I'm truly sorry."

"Not your fault, Paul. I'm sure you'll do a good job. That's what matters."

Mason angrily shucked off the last of the glue on his face and turned around, still hidden behind his men.

"Just one more matter to take care of," Knoll said. "Mrs. Armstrong, LeMarcus, the judge has a busy schedule. He needs to know whether to wait here for your client to make the required bail agreement appearance. How long will it take to have him report to the police station?"

Mason strode past Bishop and Dalton to the chair that *Christopher Johnson* had vacated earlier and sat. "You wanted to see me?"

Chapter Eleven

Hannah endured another bone-crunching hug from her mom in her parents' foyer. She and her father had barely made it through the front door before her sisters and mother converged on them. If this was how they reacted after being told she *hadn't* been kidnapped, she probably wouldn't survive if she actually *had*.

"Help," Hannah silently mouthed to her sisters over her mom's shoulder. "Can't. Breathe."

Mary giggled.

Sarah gave her a smug *serves-you-right* look, but finally relented. "Come on, Mom. Your enthusiasm is about to kill your baby. I think you've broken at least three ribs already."

Her mom gave her one last hug, then reluctantly let go, wiping at her tears. "I'm just relieved you're okay. We've been worried sick."

"I know, and I'm so, *so* sorry. Everything happened really fast. Thinking about how it would impact you all didn't even enter my mind until later. But I promise, I never meant to hurt you with my lies."

"It's okay, sweetheart." Her mother looped her arm

through Hannah's and tugged her from the foyer into the family room with her sisters and dad following. "I couldn't be prouder of you for standing up for what's right. You're a real hero."

Mary plopped down on one of the two couches. "*I'm* proud of her for snagging a real hottie. I hear that Mason Ford's ten times sexier than his brother Wyatt. And that's saying something. Wyatt's an 8, maybe even a strong 9. What's Mason, a 20?"

Hannah's face heated. "I didn't *snag* anyone."

Her mother shook her head at Mary. "Stop teasing her. I'm being serious."

"So am I." Mary grinned as Sarah sat on the opposite end of the couch. Their dad rolled his eyes from the other couch.

Her mother joined him, leaving Hannah no choice but to sit between her troublemaking sisters. They were both winking and grinning as if they were still in high school instead of married, and in Sarah's case, a mom.

"Hannah, dear," her mother said, "your dad mentioned something on the phone about Mr. Ford getting bail. Is he heading back to Tennessee? He lives in Gatlinburg, right?"

"He can't leave town," her father told her. "Condition of bail."

"Oh, I guess that makes sense. Well, I can't imagine him staying with that awful family of his. Where *is* your Mr. Ford, Hannah?"

She gritted her teeth as her sisters grinned. "He's not *my* Mr. Ford. There's nothing going on between us."

Sarah leaned in close. "But you wish there was."

Hannah shoved her but Sarah only laughed.

"Settle down, children." Since the order came from their father, they straightened up. But Mary couldn't resist one last salacious wink, with her face turned so her father couldn't see her of course.

Hannah shook her head in exasperation.

"Maybe we should offer him one of our guest rooms," her mother said.

Hannah blinked. "I don't think he—"

"He could stay with Hannah," Sarah interrupted. "She's got plenty of room. Don't you, sis?"

"Why, yes. I do, Sarah." She gave her sister a warning look, before turning to her mom. "But since he owns a cottage near the historic district, I don't think he'll be homeless anytime soon. That is, if he really is out on bail. At the end of the meeting with the DA, there was a revelation of sorts and the DA was ticked. He ordered everyone out of the squad room except for Mason, his lawyers and the judge. Dad and I don't know what happened after that."

"Oh dear," her mother said. "I do hope they worked out the problem." She patted Hannah's father's hand. "I'm sure one of your officers will get the scoop and call you with an update soon."

His face flushed and he tugged at his collar.

Hannah's mother narrowed her eyes suspiciously. "What's going on?"

He blinked. "What do you mean?"

"Don't give me that innocent look. You're hiding something. There's more to this business with Mason Ford than you've told us."

He sighed heavily. "I'm not trying to hide anything, Rachel. I was just waiting for a better time to tell you. These past few days have been emotional for all of us. I didn't want to dump bad news on you right now."

She made a disgusted face. "Mitchel James Landry. Since when have I been a delicate flower to wilt at the first hint of trouble? I've been a cop's wife most of my life, kissing you goodbye every morning and praying you'd come home safely. There's nothing worse you can throw at me than that. I can handle anything"

"Yeah, well, maybe not this."

Hannah bit her lip, knowing what he was about to say. Her heart ached as her father took her mother's hands in his.

"Rachel, honey, my career in law enforcement is over. I got fired."

Her mother burst into tears.

"Ah, honey. Don't cry." He pulled her against him and rested his chin on the top of her head.

Hannah exchanged a miserable glance with her sisters. *It's my fault*, she mouthed silently, a single tear sliding down her cheek. But rather than look outraged, they did what they always did when one of them was hurting—gave her their love and support. They sandwiched her between them and put their arms around her shoulders. The three musketeers, one for all, and all for one. She'd never been more grateful for the gift of her sisters than at this moment.

Her father shot her a helpless look and rubbed his hand up and down her mother's back. "I'm sorry, honey. I may not like what happened, but the mayor was right to let me go. Helping a fugitive escape and covering it up, well, obviously that's not something that should be tolerated in a chief of police. But, like Hannah, my conscience is at peace. We both did what we felt, and still feel, was the right thing to do. But hurting you is the last thing I ever wanted."

"Hurting me?" Her mother pushed out of his arms. "I'd despaired that this day might never come. I've been after you to retire since I retired from teaching ten years ago. But just when I thought you might finally agree, the Beauchamp mayor recruited you to move back here to try to straighten out this corrupt little town. I bet I cried for a week when you said yes."

He stared at her. "You cried? I never knew that."

"Because I didn't want you to know. Your job is to protect others. Mine is to protect you, to be supportive so you can save lives without worrying about me. But it's well past time you quit working so hard. We deserve to spend our golden years together."

"Golden years? We're not *that* old."

"Old enough. And the longer you're in law enforcement the worse the odds are that you'll get shot or seriously hurt. It's a relief that you won't be going back. I'm absolutely thrilled."

"I'm relieved that you're not upset like I thought you'd be. But, Rachel, honey, I don't know that we have enough in savings to do the things you'll want to do during our retirement. I should probably try to get a security guard job for a while or—"

"No, Mitch. You're not getting some job you're way overqualified for. We'll make do on my teacher's pension and your 401K and limit ourselves to whatever we can afford to do. As long as we have each other, we have all we need."

He gave her a skeptical look. "I've only been un-employed for a few hours. I'm not ready to make life-altering decisions about our future just yet."

"We'll figure it out together, starting tomorrow morning. Instead of leaving the house at the crack of dawn for work, you can catch up on some sleep. And when you're all rested and ready to face the day, I'll have a big old-fashioned breakfast waiting for you."

He cocked his head. "Eggs, bacon, biscuits?"

"And homemade gravy. Oh, and baked red-potato slices with onions and cheese. Your favorite."

"Darlin', you start feeding me like that and you'll have to roll me out of bed. I won't be able to move. But I sure will enjoy it." He kissed her and pulled her against his side.

"Are we invited to this amazing breakfast you're cooking tomorrow?" Sarah teased.

"You bring those adorable grandchildren of ours and I'll cook anything you want."

Sarah winced. "Thanks for that reminder. Daniel's got to be pulling his hair out with the kids about now. When I heard about Hannah, I headed out of there so fast I'm not even sure I said goodbye." She hugged Hannah's shoulders. "Now that I know she's okay, I'm going to head home before my husband files for divorce. But if that breakfast offer extends to the weekend, we'll bring the kids over then."

"That would be wonderful," her mom exclaimed.

"Mary, what about you and Ian? Can you come too? You could bring those gorgeous retrievers. I haven't seen my fur-grandbabies in ages."

"Of course. It'll be fun. I need to head home now too, but this weekend is definitely a date." She hugged Hannah tight. "I'm so proud of you and Daddy for standing up for what's right." She crossed to the other couch and hugged their dad. "The mayor's an idiot to let you go. As far as I'm concerned, he doesn't deserve you, so good riddance."

"I second that." Sarah hugged him, then grabbed her purse from the end table. "You give us his address. I'll bring the toilet paper. We'll do his house up as pretty as you please."

Her mother gasped. "Sarah, don't you dare. None of you had better dare. Please tell me you've never actually done anything like that before."

Hannah laughed. "The stories we could tell."

"I don't think I want to know. Go on. I don't want the husbands mad that we kept you so long."

"I think I'll head out too," Hannah said. "I'd like to be in my own space to unwind after all this."

"Do what you need to do. But come back this weekend to celebrate your father's retirement."

"Hey," her dad complained. "I haven't agreed that I'm retiring just yet. I have to think on it."

She patted his hand. "Of course you do, dear. But we're still celebrating this weekend."

He chuckled. "I'm on to you, Rachel. You just want me fat and lazy so I never leave home again."

"Clever man." She kissed his cheek.

Hannah was relieved at how things were turning out. But after the goodbyes were said and she stepped outside with her sisters to leave, she suddenly realized that she didn't have a car. An officer had driven her and her dad home because he had to turn in his police-issued SUV. And her Tucson was still parked in Mason's barn.

Mary waved as she backed out of the driveway, then drove away.

Sarah was about to get in her car, when she looked around. "Where's your Tucson?"

"Actually, I just realized I haven't gotten it back from Mason since the, ah—"

"Fake kidnapping?"

She sighed. "Yeah. That. I'll head back inside and have a rental sent over. I don't want to take mom, and dad's car."

"No way. I can drive you home."

"It would add an hour to your trip since it's in the opposite direction of where you need to go. Besides, I need the rental anyway. There's no telling when I'll see Mason again and be able to get my car. I'd prefer to get the rental rather than be stranded at my house without transportation." When her sister hesitated, Hannah hugged her. "I'm a big girl. I've got this. Go. Give my favorite niece and nephew a hug, and kiss that sexy brother-in-law of mine. I'll see you all soon."

"I bet when Mary has kids, you'll tell her the same thing about them being your favorite."

"Probably. But Daniel will always be cuter than Ian."

Sarah laughed. "You're right about that. Take care, little sister. Call if you need me."

"Always."

After watching Sarah drive away, Hannah went back inside. Her parents were still on the couch, her mom's head against her dad's shoulder. They looked so content it made her heart swell with happiness instead of the guilt that had been consuming her.

"Car wouldn't start?" her dad asked. "Oh, wait. You don't have a car. Goodness me, I totally forgot. I'll get my keys and—"

A knock sounded on the door.

"Stay there. I'll get it." Hannah returned to the foyer and opened the door. Her stomach did a little flip when she saw who was there. "Um, hi."

"Hi yourself." Mason smiled, looking unbelievably sexy in a chic, linen suit that had to have been tailored for him to hug his broad shoulders so well. His team must have brought some of his clothes with them from Tennessee. Or maybe he'd gone back to his barn-apartment and gotten something. Either way, she definitely approved.

"*Good grief*, you look good."

His answering grin and knowing wink had her face turning warm.

"So do you. Always. I hope you don't mind that I'm here. I asked around at the station and was told an officer drove you and your dad to this address. It's your father's place, right?"

"It is. Mine's half an hour from here."

"And you don't have your Tucson because it's in my barn." He motioned toward the Altima parked in the driveway. "Rather conveniently, I have a car and would love to drive you home. That is, if you're not staying here."

"Honey, who is it?" her father called out.

She leaned past the doorway to see around the foyer wall. "It's Mason, Daddy."

"Well ask him in."

She turned back to Mason. "I'd love a ride. That was really nice of you to come all the way out here. But, um, would you mind coming in for just a minute? Otherwise I'll get lectured on my bad manners."

"Well we wouldn't want that." He winked again and stepped inside.

When she introduced him to her mom, she fairly swooned. Hannah couldn't believe her mother was blushing, or that Mason actually kissed the back of her hand like an old-world gentleman. Not only was he funny and clever and sexy, he knew how to turn on the charm. Thank goodness her sisters weren't here or they'd have teased her mercilessly, or fawned all over him like her mother was doing right now. She met her father's laughing gaze. He shrugged, obviously finding her mother's behavior amusing.

"I stopped by to offer Hannah a ride home because I still have her car," Mason told them. "But I also wanted to thank you, Chief Landry."

Her father winced at the title, but Mason continued.

"Very few people would have done what you and your daughter did. You both saved my life. And in return, you lost your job, your career, your livelihood. I owe you a debt I can never repay. But I hope this helps make up for your tremendous loss."

He pulled an envelope out of his suit jacket pocket and handed it to her father.

He frowned as he opened it and pulled out a piece of paper. His gaze shot to Mason's. "A check?"

"I know it's impersonal, but it's all I can do right now to try to make up for what happened."

He held the check toward Mason. "I didn't help you for financial gain. And even if I had, this would be way too much. I can't accept this."

"I don't think you understand, sir. By accepting that check, you're doing me a favor. You're helping assuage some of my guilt for the harm that helping me did to you and your family. My company's mission is to assist people in law enforcement who lose their jobs while trying to do the right thing. You're the poster example of that." He motioned toward the check her father was still holding. "That's no more than I'd give one of my Seekers as a typical signing bonus. It's my way of thanking them for their service. It's an honor to be able to do the same for you."

"Mason." He cleared his throat, his voice raw. "I appreciate what you're trying to do. But I can't—"

Hannah's mom grabbed the check and looked at it. Her eyes widened in shock. "Yes, Mitch. You *can*. Do you realize what this means for us? You can retire without worrying whether we've saved enough. We can travel and check off both our bucket lists. It's a miracle. Don't you dare give it back."

Mason smiled. "Your wife is a wise woman, Chief. I suggest you follow her advice. And please don't worry about the amount. I can easily afford it."

Her father frowned. "Rachel, I thought you said as long as we had each other, that's all we needed."

Her mother's cheeks took on a rosy hue. "That's still true. But it doesn't mean that extra money wouldn't make things a whole lot easier, and more fun." She handed him the check. "It's your decision. I won't be mad either way. But I think you're crazy if you say no."

He laughed, then handed it back to her. "For safekeeping."

Her smile lit up the entire room.

Her father shook Mason's hand. "You've made my wife happy. There's no better gift than that."

Hannah leaned against Mason's side and hugged him. He smiled down at her before meeting her dad's gaze. "There *is* one more thing, sir. I would appreciate it if you and your wife would leave town for a while. Take a vacation. My treat. All expenses paid."

Her father eyed him warily. "Why?"

"A precaution. Abrams and Donnelly have escaped."

Hannah sucked in a breath. "What happened?"

"That's what I want to know," her father said.

"I don't have many details. The DA and I were finishing our meeting when Murphy sent for them so that Special Agent Holland could conduct an interview. An officer came running into the squad room a few minutes later, saying one of the guards was hurt and the prisoners were gone."

Hannah noted the worry lines on both men's faces. Her mother looked pale.

"Why are you concerned that they'd come after my parents? Dad didn't do anything to them."

"I had them arrested. We've had run-ins before, on other cases. They're a tight-knit pair and seem to egg each other on. I've reprimanded both of them in the past. If they're desperate, and out for revenge, I can see them coming after me. It wouldn't be the first time a criminal blamed the man who caught him instead of taking responsibility for his own actions." He kissed her mom. "Honey, how about pack us a bag. Just enough for a few days. We can stop back for more later if it looks like we'll be gone for a long time."

"A vacation sounds good to me. I can ask my friend Martha to come over and water the plants while we're gone. Hannah, can you let Sarah and Mary know we have to postpone the weekend plans? Maybe you can all come see us wherever we land."

"Sure, Mom. Whatever you need."

"Thanks, Hannah. Dear, I'll have us packed in ten minutes." She hurried down the hallway to their bedroom.

Her father pulled out his cell phone. "I imagine I've still got allies at the office. I'll get a status on the search for our two escapees." He opened the sliding glass door and stepped onto the back deck.

Hannah took one of Mason's hands in hers. "If they're out for revenge, you could be a target too. They risked everything to frame you, and yet it was your security video that brought them down."

"I agree. It's one of the reasons I wanted to see you. How would you like to stay with me for a while?"

She blinked, a delicious heat spreading through her. "*Stay* with you?"

He took both her hands in his, threading their fingers together. "I'm going to lie low until these two fools are caught. My lawyer's renting an estate outside of town for my team and me. One of the Seekers is setting up security right now. There's a guesthouse on the property, a good distance from the main house." He cleared his throat. "It's easily big enough for two."

Her fingers jerked in his as she drew a shaky breath.

As if unable to resist the temptation, he pressed a whisper-soft kiss against her forehead, before pulling back. She shivered in response.

"Tell me if I'm reading the signals wrong," he said. "But I believe that you and I have a connection, something special, rare, something that could be..." He shook his head as if struggling for the right words. "I want to explore this...bond, this attraction, whatever it is between us. I'm asking if you'll share the guesthouse with me, at least until Abrams and Donnelly are rounded up again. Maybe even for the duration of the investigation, if you want. It's definitely what I want. Assuming you don't tire of me." He gently feathered her hair back from her face. "This shouldn't be happening, with everything else going on. It's the last thing that should be consuming my thoughts, keeping me awake at night—"

"What's keeping you awake at night?" Her voice was barely above a whisper as she stared up into his beautiful, incredibly expressive eyes.

He cupped her face in his hands. "*You*, sweet Hannah. You're what keeps me up at night. I'm falling for you. Please tell me I'm not the only one."

She stepped close, reveling in the heat of his body.

Craving the feel of his skin against hers. Wanting more, so much more, but well aware that either of her parents could walk in at any moment. She settled on smoothing her hands up the front of his shirt, caressing the hard contours of his chest. "Mason?"

"Yes?" His voice was a deep rasp of need.

"You're not the only one."

He let out a ragged breath, tightening his arms around her. Ever so slowly, he leaned down, angling his mouth toward hers. Closer, closer. The tension built between them until she thought she might scream if he didn't kiss her, *right now.*

Bam!

He grabbed her and dived to the floor, his body wrapped protectively around hers.

Bam! Bam!

She stared up at him in shock. "Gunshots?"

"Rifle fire." He shook his head in disgust. "And I don't have a gun because of the bail agreement." He raised up, looking toward the front windows.

"Mason, my purse. You can use my gun." She looked around, trying to remember where she'd left it.

He scrambled onto his knees and peered over the back of the couch. "Hannah, stay here. Don't move."

"Wait, I'm getting the gun." She reached for her purse on the end table but Mason didn't wait. He took off running toward the back of the house. *The back of the house?* Her father!

She shoved to her feet and ran past the hallway just as her mother ran out of the bedroom. Hannah stumbled to a halt.

"Did I hear shooting?" Her mother's eyes were wide with fear.

"Mason's checking it out. Go back in the bedroom, Mom, please. Get down on the floor."

Hannah ran to the back door, then pressed her hand to her throat. Her father was lying on the deck, not moving, blood saturating his hair, his shirt. Mason was kneeling beside him, pressing his wadded up suit jacket against her father's wounds.

She jerked open the sliding glass door so hard it slammed against the frame and bounced back against her. She shoved it back again. "*Daddy*. Mason, what—"

"Call 911."

So much blood. Oh God. Daddy. Daddy. She started shaking. Spots swam in front of her eyes.

"Hannah!"

She jumped at his shout, frowning in confusion. "What are you— He can't— I don't— *Daddy*—"

"Hannah. Listen to me. Your dad's been shot. Do you understand?"

She blinked, then nodded. "Yes, he—"

"I've got to keep pressure on the wounds. I need you to call 911. Hurry!"

His words galvanized her into action. She ran inside and grabbed her phone.

"Hannah?" Mason yelled again.

She sprinted to the back door, phone in hand.

His agonized gaze met hers. "Tell them to send a chopper."

Chapter Twelve

Mason straightened his tie and tugged his latest suit jacket into place outside the main entrance to the surgical waiting room. Alexandria's Rapides Regional Medical Center was the closest level one trauma center to Beauchamp, but it had still been an hour and a half's drive. Thankfully, the medical chopper got Landry here much faster than that. He was in surgery long before Hannah and her mother arrived, followed by her sisters. Mason had been delayed because he'd had to get special permission from the DA to leave the parish. Since Al was seated about ten feet from Hannah's family, it was a good thing he'd taken that extra precaution. Otherwise, Al would probably arrest him. He still might try if Mason didn't head him off.

A quick glance confirmed that Dalton and Bryson were inside the waiting room, discreetly keeping watch. But he didn't see his newest Seeker, Eli. He was supposed to come here after bringing Mason a fresh suit that wasn't covered with blood.

The sound of voices down the long main hallway had Mason looking that way. Eli was facing him, talking to a dark-haired man with his back to Mason. He seemed familiar, but at this distance, without being able to see his face, Mason didn't have a clue who he was. When Eli spotted him, he said something else to the man, then hurried over.

"Hey, boss. The suit looks good."

"I appreciate you bringing it." He motioned toward the stranger who was continuing down the hall away from them. "Was there a problem?"

"What?" He glanced where Mason had gestured. "Oh. Just some guy asking for directions to the men's room. I'd just come back from there myself so I knew where it was." He looked toward the waiting room, then back at Mason. "Bryson and Dalton knew I was leaving. Is…is that okay?"

"Of course." Mason smiled reassuringly, hating the twinge of suspicion just because his newest Seeker, and fellow Louisianan, was talking to someone he didn't recognize. Not knowing the *whys* and *whos* behind Audrey's murder and the frame-up had him leery about trusting anyone he didn't know all that well. Eli certainly fell into that category, having only been on the team for a few months.

"Have you seen Bishop? I called him from the DA's office and asked him to act as bodyguard for Landry."

Eli grinned. "Bishop's in surgery."

"*In* surgery?"

"He told the doctors that he's not leaving Landry's side and they'd better make sure the chief pulls through or he'll hold them personally accountable. They had him scrub up and gown up. And since you somehow convinced the hospital administrator to honor our concealed carry permits inside the building, Bishop's even packing in the OR. His pistol is wrapped in sterile plastic, but he still has it on him."

Somehow had been a generous donation in Mitch Landry's name. Heck, they might even name a wing of the hospital after him as a result. But the outrageous expense ensured the Seekers could conceal carry in the hospital and that they had full access to just about anywhere they needed to go. Mason had been determined to remove any barriers that could interfere with the Seekers here in Alexandria protecting the Landry family. The rest of the team was still in Beauchamp, pounding the pavement, going door-to-door, examining the evidence collected by the crime scene techs. They were doing everything possible to prove Mason's innocence.

"Thanks, Eli. Keep up the good work."

The look of relief on his face had Mason feeling even more guilty for being suspicious. But it didn't take the suspicions away.

He headed into the waiting room, nodding at Bryson and Dalton, who immediately spotted him. Hannah saw him too, and motioned for him to join her and her family. He held up a hand to let her know it would be a minute.

Al had pushed to his feet as soon as Mason walked in. His hand was hovering near the bulge beneath his suit jacket, no doubt his service weapon. Stopping in front of him, Mason handed Al his get-out-of-jail-free card, the signed agreement from the DA that said he could leave Sabine Parish for the purpose of going to and from Rapides Medical Center.

"Is this legit?" Al frowned at the paper. "I've never heard of Knoll doing this before."

"Feel free to call and check."

"Maybe I will." He handed it back and sat. But instead of taking out his phone, he crossed his arms and frowned his displeasure at the far wall.

Mason sat beside him.

Al's mouth tightened and he continued his study of the peeling wallpaper.

"I'm sorry about everything that's happened, Al. I meant no disrespect to you or anyone else at Beauchamp PD. But when your life's on the line, you'll do almost anything to survive."

"Yeah, well. Apparently that includes not trusting old friends. And bringing in a lot of outsiders who think they're better than the rest of us."

"Not better. Different. And can you blame me for wanting people by my side who aren't from Beauchamp? After my family's history here, including *recent* history? Honestly?"

Al sighed heavily. "You make it dang hard to hold a grudge."

Mason held out his hand. "Truce?"

Al smiled reluctantly and shook his hand. "Truce. As long as you keep me in the loop going forward and don't pull any more stunts."

"I'll keep you in the loop as much as possible. And I'll only pull a stunt if someone's life is in danger and I don't feel I have another choice. Fair enough?"

"Fair enough." He motioned toward Hannah and her family. "They're glaring daggers at me like they think I'm about to arrest you. I can only imagine what would happen if I tried. Go on. They don't pay me to sit and gab with murder suspects." He smiled, letting Mason know he was teasing. Partly, at least.

Instead of joining Hannah, Mason crossed to Dalton and leaned down so no one would overhear. "Eli was out in the hall talking to a dark-haired man in jeans and a blue blazer a few minutes ago. Have you seen that guy?"

"No. Is he someone you know?"

"Not sure. He seemed familiar but he was far away and I didn't see his face. Eli swears he was a stranger needing directions."

"Height? Weight?"

"Six foot one, tops. Weight's hard to judge because of the blazer but he had an athletic build, smaller than me."

"I'll check around, see if some of the nurses or other patients spotted him."

"Thanks, Dalton. Be discreet. It's probably nothing, and I don't want Eli thinking I suspect him of something."

"But you do?"

He shrugged. "I'm being extra cautious."

Dalton clasped his shoulder. "I've got this." He stood and crossed to Bryson. After whispering to him for a moment, Dalton left the waiting room.

Mason headed to the corner of the room to greet Hannah and her family. His heart nearly broke when he saw the tears in their eyes and the stark fear etched in their expressions. After a quick greeting to all of them, he knelt in front of Rachel Landry so they were at eye level.

"Mrs. Landry, is there anything I can do for you? Anything you need while you wait for word on your husband?"

She twisted a tissue in her lap. "You saw him, after he was…you saw him. I haven't talked to any doctors. No one will tell me anything. The volunteer at the desk over there will only say he's still in surgery. How bad is it? Do you think…do you think he'll make it?"

Hannah touched her shoulder. "Mama, don't ask him something like—"

"It's okay." He smiled at her, then took her mother's hands in his. "I'll tell you what I do know, Mrs. Landry. I know that your husband has a reputation for being an honorable, devoted family man who loves you and your daughters very much. I've also heard he's a fighter, fighting for what he believes in, for what he knows is right and for what matters most to him. *You're* what matters most. I know that he won't give up, and he'll do everything he can to try to come back to you."

She let out a sob and reached for him. He pulled her close, letting her cry against his shoulder as he gently rocked her back and forth. Hannah and her sisters smiled through their tears. He hated that they were all going through such agony. They were good people. They didn't deserve this. No one did.

After she'd calmed down, she moved to sit between Sarah and Mary and closed her eyes with her head on Mary's shoulder. Mason took the seat she'd vacated and sat beside Hannah, holding her hand while they waited for news. Sarah smiled at the two of them, then laid her head back and closed her eyes.

Another hour went by before the volunteer that Mrs. Landry had mentioned gave them an update. Essentially it was the same as before, that he was still in surgery. But that meant he was still alive. And where there was life, there was hope.

Paul Murphy walked into the waiting room a few minutes later. He spoke quietly to Al before coming over. Hannah stiffened. Mason squeezed her hand and straightened in his chair.

"Mr. Ford, Hannah." He greeted her sisters, then smiled sadly at their mom. "Mrs. Landry, I want you to know that everyone at the station is pulling for your husband. It's been an honor working for him these past few years. I've certainly learned a lot. If it was in my power, I'd reinstate him immediately, and I know I'm not the only one who feels that way."

Her chin wobbled and she gave Hannah a helpless look.

Hannah cleared her throat, getting his attention. "My mother appreciates your sentiments, Paul. But she can't talk right now. It's too hard."

"I understand. My apologies if my being here puts additional stress on you all. I want you to know that we're working hard to find out who's responsible for what happened to Chief Landry. The obvious suspects are the deputies who escaped. But we're not jumping to conclusions. We're exploring every lead."

He motioned to Al, who was watching them. "Detective Latimer would like to ask you some questions about what happened while it's still fresh in your minds. He's been waiting, out of respect for what you're going through. But we really need to jump on this. Which of you saw what happened to the Chief?"

"No one." Mason said. "He was on the back deck. Mary and Sarah had already left when it happened. The shots were fired while Mrs. Landry was in her bedroom. Hannah and I were in the main room. Neither of us saw the shooters. We only saw the aftermath. But I did hear tires squealing right after the shooting, so it seems likely it was a drive-by."

Paul's expression mirrored his disappointment. "You didn't see the vehicle?"

"No. I couldn't even tell you which direction they were going, though obviously they had to drive down the street that runs behind the Landry home in order to have a line of sight into the backyard. If you haven't already, I recommend you canvass the neighborhood for any doorbell security videos or other home security cameras. Check out businesses within a five-mile radius for surveillance cameras to determine what vehicles were in the vicinity shortly after the time of the shooting. You might get lucky and trace some license plates to potential suspects."

"I think we're already doing all that, but I'll put a bug in Al's ear to be sure. How soon after the shooting did someone call 911?"

"I'd say one to two minutes." He glanced at Hannah. "Does that seem right?"

"A shot rang out. You tackled me to the floor to protect me just as two more shots sounded. I swear you were on the back deck within seconds of that."

"Who called 911?" Murphy asked.

"I did," Hannah said. "Mason was helping my father, trying to stop the bleeding." Her mother's face blanched. Hannah reached across Mason to squeeze her arm.

Mason met Murphy's gaze. "You're looking for a rifle, guarantee it. There's no mistaking that sound."

"Good to know. There were three shots? With a pause in between the first and the rest?"

"That's my recollection. Hannah?"

"Yes. One shot, a pause, then two more."

"Is there anything else you can add?" Murphy asked. "Is there any point in sending Al over to question you?"

Hannah shook her head no.

"I'll add one thing," Mason said. "Chief Landry was on the back deck, alone, talking on the phone for several minutes before the shooting happened. They don't have a fence around their property, nothing obstructing the view. Whoever pulled the trigger knew exactly who they were shooting."

Murphy shook Mason's hand. "Thank you. I'll relay the information to Al. And we'll let all of you know as soon as we have anything substantive in this investigation."

No sooner had Murphy left, taking Al with him, than a doctor in green scrubs entered the waiting room. He spoke to the volunteer at the information desk. She pointed them out, but instead of coming over, the doctor told her something else and left. She rounded the desk and started across the room toward them.

Hannah clutched Mason's hand, her expression filled with dread as she and her family prepared themselves for whatever they were about to hear. Mason knew that look, knew that feeling. He also knew the soul-shattering blow of being told that a family member hadn't made it. He prayed that Hannah and her family weren't about to receive that devastating news.

The lady stopped in front of them, her polite smile as benign and difficult to interpret as the *Mona Lisa*'s. "Mrs. Landry, Doctor Stanton would like to speak in private to you and your family about your husband."

Chapter Thirteen

Hannah sat with her mom and sisters in the tiny meeting room as Doctor Stanton gave them the update they'd both wanted and dreaded. Mason leaned against the far wall. He'd offered to give them privacy and wait outside, but they'd all emphatically told him they wanted him there. Hannah felt it was a testament to his strength and kindness that he was the rock her family was leaning on, even though they barely knew him. She, of course, felt like she'd known him for years. And so far, every wonderful thing that Olivia had said about him had proven to be true.

"I don't understand," her mother said, her voice raw. "His *ribs* are broken?"

Sarah patted her hand. "If you'll quit interrupting him, maybe it will all make sense, Mama."

Stanton looked at them over the top of his glasses. "I know this can be confusing."

"Can you start over, please?" Hannah asked. "I think we're all having trouble with the medical terms you're throwing out."

"Sure. I'll try to summarize it without the jargon.

Mr. Landry made it through surgery without any major complications. After he leaves recovery, he'll be moved to intensive care for around-the-clock monitoring. The bullets nicked his spleen, left kidney and fractured a couple of ribs. There was a lot of bleeding from the head wound as well as the internal injuries so we had to give him several pints of blood. Whoever called for the medical chopper no doubt saved his life. If he'd gotten here a few minutes later, I honestly don't think we could have saved him."

Hannah smiled her gratitude at Mason, then caught her mother's confused glance. "What is it, Mom?"

"The gunshot wound to his head. He didn't talk about it other than the bleeding." She clutched her ever-present tissues. "Is he…will he ever be the same again? Will he wake up?" Her voice broke and Mary hugged her close.

"I'm so sorry if I gave you the impression that he was shot in the head. He wasn't. The head injuries, based on what the EMTs relayed about the scene, were likely a result of him slamming his head against the deck when he fell. His scalp was lacerated and bled extensively. He's got a concussion, and there's a possibility his brain could swell. But we'll monitor him closely and act quickly if the worst happens."

Her mother blinked. "The worst? What does that mean?"

"Poor choice of words on my part. There are many things that can go wrong. Your husband suffered serious injuries and will need rehabilitation in order to make a full recovery. But while I can't make any promises, I'm optimistic he'll make a full recovery."

Her mother's expression still seemed confused, but there was also something else there. Hope. "Are you… are you saying he's going to be okay?"

"I'm saying he has an excellent chance of being okay, yes, ma'am."

She covered her face and started crying again.

While Hannah's sisters comforted her mother, she shook the doctor's hand. "Thank you so much, Doctor Stanton. When can we see my father?"

"You can head to the ICU waiting area now. As soon as he's in a room, someone will let you know."

The long wait was excruciating, but finally they were brought to the ICU to her father's room. Seeing him lying there, still unconscious, hooked up to monitors broke Hannah's heart. He was alarmingly pale. Wires and tubes formed a spiderweb around him. But he was alive. The doctor was optimistic. And it was all because of Mason that her father had made it this far.

While her mother and sisters hovered by his bedside, Hannah pulled Mason to the other side of the room by the door.

He looked down at her, his brows raised in question. She cupped his face and stood on tiptoe to give him a quick kiss. As she pulled back, his lips curved in a surprised, but achingly sweet smile.

"What was that for?" he whispered.

Her heart was full as she looked up at him. "Thank you. Thank you for running outside to help my father even though the shooters could have still been there. Thank you for working tirelessly to keep him from bleeding out before help could arrive. Thank you for somehow knowing exactly what to say to reach me through my panic and getting me to call 911. And thank you, thank God for you, that you knew to request the helicopter so we didn't lose time waiting for an ambulance, only to realize the chopper was needed. Mason, there's no question that my father would be dead right now if it wasn't for you. *Thank you.*"

She kissed him again.

"I'd ask for one of those too, but Daniel might not like it."

Hannah jerked back at the sound of Sarah's voice.

Sarah smiled through her tears and put her arms around Mason, giving him a tight hug. His eyes widened in surprise, but he hugged her back. When she let go, she rolled her eyes at Hannah. "Stop looking so jealous. It's obvious who puts that spark in his eyes. And it's not me."

Hannah felt her face heat. Sarah laughed and put her arms around her shoulders. "Thank you, Mason. I heard what Hannah said and I second it 1,000 percent. So do Mom and Mary. We know how lucky we are to still have our father with us. No, not *lucky.* Fortunate, and grateful that you were there to save him."

He shook his head. "I don't deserve such praise, but I'm honored just the same."

Sarah started to say something else, but a knock sounded on the door.

Mason gently pushed them behind him, once again being the fierce protector even though he had two men stationed outside the door to watch over them. Let alone one of Beauchamp PD's officers by the nurse's desk watching out for Donnelly, Abrams or anyone else who might intend her father harm.

After opening the door a crack and speaking to someone, he gave Hannah a surprised look. "Do you and your family feel like having a visitor?"

"A visitor? Who?"

"My sister. Olivia."

AFTER A BRIEF greeting with his sister, Mason stepped out of the room so she could visit Hannah and her family. Dalton was leaning against the far wall and subtly motioned toward the nurse's desk a short distance away. There, speaking to one of the nurses, was the man Mason had seen earlier with Eli. Same dark hair, jeans and blue jacket. But this close, Mason realized the man wasn't just familiar.

He was his brother. Wyatt.

Chapter Fourteen

Mason leaned against the far wall beside Dalton, watching his brother flirt with one of the nurses at the nursing station. "Looks like you found the guy who was talking to Eli."

Dalton arched a brow. "Looks a lot like you."

"I never thought so, growing up. My older brother, Landon, was practically my twin."

"And the woman who was with him?"

"Baby sister. Olivia. There were six of us—Landon, me, Ava, Charlotte…" He nodded toward the nurse's desk. "And Wyatt."

His brother laughed at whatever the nurse had said, then started across the hall toward Landry's room. Bishop shifted his weight, blocking the door.

Wyatt put his hands on his hips. "Hey, man. Do you mind? I need to get in there."

Bishop pointed across the hall.

Wyatt looked over his shoulder, then slowly turned around. He hesitated, then with a noticeable lack of enthusiasm, closed the distance between them. "Mason."

"Wyatt. You don't seem surprised to see me in Louisiana."

He hooked his fingers into the belt loops on his jeans. "Considering your name was all over the news for kidnapping someone, can't say that I am. Wanted for murder too. *Audrey's* murder. Now *that* was a surprise. Chief Ford, a common criminal. Who knew you could ever fall so low." He motioned toward the Beauchamp police officer sitting a short distance away. "I assume he's taking you back to jail after you finish doing whatever you were brought here to do?"

Dalton stiffened. Bishop took a step forward, as if to intervene, but Mason subtly shook his head.

"I've missed you too, Wyatt. How's your financial advisor business these days?"

He frowned. "Aren't you even going to deny the charges? Protest your innocence?"

"Would it matter if I did?"

Wyatt swore. "Nothing ever shakes your calm, does it? I know you wouldn't kidnap anyone and you certainly would never hurt Audrey. Heck, I doubt you'd cross a street unless you were at the corner with the walking sign flashing."

His brother would be shocked to know what lines he'd cross these days for true justice. But at least his brother didn't believe he was a murderer. "Then why do you seem so aggravated? What's the problem?"

"Problem?" His jaw clenched. "The grapevine says a couple of corrupt deputies abducted you and forcibly brought you here, then set you up to be charged for murder. And it never occurred to you to ask your own brother for help? Or call your family and tell us what was going on?"

"I was too busy trying not to get killed to worry about catching up."

He rolled his eyes. "What *is* going on? And why are you here, outside Chief Landry's room, instead of in jail?"

Mason debated telling him anything. His brother had rarely ever expressed concern for him in the past. But he relented and told him the nickel version of what had happened.

Wyatt winced. "That's just crazy. I'm glad the DA seems to be working with you, though. And let you out on bail." He motioned toward Dalton. "Is he one of your *Justice Seekers*, here to rescue you?"

Dalton pushed away from the wall and offered his hand. "The name's Dalton Lynch."

Wyatt shook his hand.

Instead of letting go, Dalton held on, until Wyatt met his gaze. "I'm a very good friend of your brother's, as well as his employee. As for rescuing, he took care of that himself. He also rescued Chief Landry, saved his life. *That's* why he's here, in the hospital." He let go, and leaned back against the wall.

Wyatt eyed him as if he was a rattlesnake and had just bitten him. From the way their knuckles had whitened when they'd shaken hands, Mason imagined there'd been some kind of challenge going on. There was no question that Dalton had won.

"Behind you," Mason said, "guarding the Chief's door is Bishop. Another good friend. Also a Seeker."

Wyatt held out his hand. Bishop crossed his arms.

His face reddening, Wyatt turned back to Mason. "Real friendly fellas."

"The best."

Wyatt shook his head, clearly exasperated.

"Now that you know why I'm here, why are *you* here? Hannah didn't mention that she knew you. Are you friends of one of the other Landrys? Or is Olivia having another bad spell?"

"Hannah? You're on a first name basis with the chief's daughter? You don't waste time, do you?"

If Wyatt could have seen the deadly look in Bishop's eyes behind him, he'd probably have taken off running. Mason didn't answer his brother's childish question.

His brother sighed. "Yes, Olivia's having a tough time. I try to give her space. She's got her own suite of rooms at my house. But I watch over her, check on her. It's what family does. They stick together."

Ignoring his latest gibe, especially since it was his family's choice to ignore him, not the other way around, he asked, "Has she been to her therapist? Is she taking her meds?"

"That's where we're going after we leave here, to her doctor. I'm going to request that he adjust her medication, at least for the short term. As soon as she heard about Hannah's dad getting shot, she lost it. Took forever to calm her down. Luckily she's not one to listen to the news or plug in to local gossip, so she hasn't heard about Audrey or what's going on with you yet. I'd appreciate it if you don't tell her any of that, at least until we've been to her doctor."

"I can't imagine Audrey's death would bother her any more than any other stranger's. She didn't like Audrey when we were together, and that's ancient history."

"So is Landon's death but that still bothers some of us."

Dalton swore under his breath.

"Wyatt," Mason said, "I'm well aware that you blame me for Landon's death because I was the chief of police and couldn't keep him from being convicted. And you blame me for Olivia's problems afterward. But this isn't the place or time to go into all of that. I just wanted to know if Olivia is okay. If there's something I can do to help, please let me know. You've been taking care of her for a long time, so I'll defer to your wishes. I won't tell her about Audrey and the charges against me until you think it's okay to do so. But I don't know if the Landrys will mention it."

Wyatt studied him a moment, then blew out a long breath. "If they tell her, I'll deal with it. You're right that she's never been a fan of Audrey. But the circumstances of Audrey's death are similar, at least at first blush, to what happened with Mandy and Landon. I'm worried the similarity could send her into a tailspin. Since she's already having trouble coping with Hannah's family troubles, adding her favorite brother's on top of that would likely send her over the edge. I'd like to avoid a hospitalization for her if I can. It's been years since we had to do that."

Mason winced. "I didn't think about it that way."

"You should have."

Dalton stepped forward, forcing Wyatt to back up

or be hit by the brim of Dalton's Stetson. "Mason's too nice and polite to stand up for himself with his so-called family. I'm not. And neither is Bishop. I suggest you either figure out how to be respectful or move down the hall, before Bishop and I lose the last of what little patience we have left with the likes of you."

Wyatt gave him a disgusted look. But he was wise enough to realize that Dalton wasn't bluffing. He crossed to one of the chairs by the police officer and sat, looking anywhere but at Mason and the others.

Mason leaned against the wall as Dalton did the same. "You know I don't need you to fight my battles."

"I know. But if he'd said one more nasty thing to you, I'd have ended up arrested. So I figure I was doing you the favor of not having to bail me out."

Mason smiled. "If you put it that way, thanks."

"No problem."

Mason eyed Wyatt's profile, wishing he knew how to heal the rift between them, a rift that had begun the moment that Landon was charged with murder. Olivia had been inconsolable and Wyatt had been the one to calm her down when their parents and sisters were wrapped up trying to help Landon, and Mason had been trying to find the real killer.

Olivia had fallen apart, and the one left to pick up the pieces was Wyatt. He'd appointed himself her guardian angel, moved her in with him, and had been performing that duty ever since. Hannah was right when she'd said Olivia was fragile. She'd been so young when Landon died, only fifteen. Now, at twenty-three, she seemed to be doing well when he spoke to her on the phone or saw her during one of her rare visits to Gatlinburg. But obviously she was struggling more than he'd realized.

When the door finally opened, both Olivia and Hannah stepped outside the room. Hannah hugged Olivia, and then Olivia hugged Mason.

"Sorry to leave before we can catch up," she said. "But I, ah, have an appointment. See you later?"

"Of course. I won't leave town without making sure I see you first."

She smiled and went to Wyatt, who led her away without a backward glance.

"Brr." Hannah rubbed her hands up and down her arms. "A bit frosty between you and your brother. And Olivia didn't seem to have a clue why you were here, so I didn't mention anything about what's happened to you. None of us did."

"I appreciate it. Wyatt's trying to keep that from her for now, to protect her. I'm sure he'll resent me even more because of it. He owns a financial investment company and has to take time off whenever Olivia needs help."

"Your other sisters can't help her? Ava and Charlotte? I remember Olivia saying they're both married and live in other towns, but couldn't they come home if Olivia needs them?"

"I suppose they could. But Wyatt and Olivia are really close. He considers it his job to take care of her."

"Well if he chooses to be the only family member to watch after her when she needs assistance, that's on him. She's got your parents and two sisters who could help. And I'm sure you would too if she reached out to you."

"I've tried to get her to move to Gatlinburg and stay with me. But she doesn't want to leave Beauchamp."

"Well there you go. Your family has made it impossible for you to live here, so you've done all you can. Stop feeling guilty."

He arched a brow. "What makes you think I feel guilty?"

"I see it in your eyes, hear it in your voice when you talk about her. Nothing that has happened to your family is your fault. I really wish you could believe that."

"Most of the time, I do. It's harder when I'm here. Ready to go back in the room to see your dad?"

"I am. But I wanted to finish that conversation we were having at my parents' house first, before…" She swallowed. "Before my father was shot. Is that offer to stay at the guesthouse with you still open?"

Heat flashed through him. He had to clear his throat before trying to talk. "Of course, but I thought you'd want to stay with your family now."

"Tonight, definitely. After that, it depends on how well he does. The nurses aren't happy with how many of us are in there with him. They want to limit the number of visitors. Mom is staying. She shut them right down when they said she couldn't. They agreed to bring in a cot for her. My sisters and I will take turns sitting with her, bringing her food and fresh clothes. Sarah and Mary will go home soon to pack bags for a longer-term stay. I know Sarah has to get a babysitter to watch her kids so her husband can go back to work. I'll need more clothes too. It's all just…so complicated. And even though I want to be here for my family, I'm itching to get into the investigation too. I want to use my degree for something really useful—finding out who shot my father and helping clear the charges against you."

He tucked a few loose strands of her hair behind her ears. "I've got a whole team working on that. You don't have to do anything."

"I want to. This is as personal for me now as it is for you. If you're worried about my safety, then include me. Let me work with you. Because if you don't, I'll investigate on my own."

"Sounds like blackmail to me."

"It's my first time being a blackmailer. How am I doing?"

He smiled. "I'd say pretty well. But I'm not sure it counts, since I'd rather have you with me anyway." He motioned toward the Beauchamp police officer, who was openly watching them. "Unfortunately, I can't stay much longer. The DA never intended for me to be here long-term. I need to return to Sabine Parish."

"Hopefully I can join you soon." She stepped close and pressed a quick kiss against his lips. "Thank you, Mason. For everything." She squeezed his hand, then headed back into her father's room.

Mason let out a ragged breath. When he felt Dalton's stare, he held up a hand to stop whatever he was going to say. "Don't make me hurt you."

"I have no idea what you're talking about." Laughter was heavy in his tone.

Mason crossed to Bishop, with Dalton following.

"I'm heading back to Beauchamp. If you don't mind standing guard tonight, I'll send Jaxon to spell you early in the morning."

"I'll stay as long as you need me."

He clasped Bishop's shoulder in thanks. "I'll update the hospital administrator to smooth the way so Jaxon can conceal carry while he's here too. Dalton, can you stand guard until Bishop gets some dinner? Then head directly to the estate?"

"No problem. As long as he doesn't take too long."

Bishop rolled his eyes and stepped away from his spot by the door so Dalton could take up his stance.

Bishop glanced at Mason as they headed down the hall. "What's happening at the estate?"

"Team meeting. I'll have someone include you by phone. We need to talk strategy, make assignments, figure out who's doing what. I want to get those bastards, Donnelly and Abrams. And figure out who murdered Audrey. It's time to catch a killer."

Chapter Fifteen

Hannah had been surprised later that week when Bishop picked her up at the hospital and said the remote property outside of town that Mason had rented was the infamous Fontenot estate. Everyone in Beauchamp had heard about this place, though few had ever seen it. *Fontenot's Folly*, as the locals called it, was rumored to be a mishmash of architectural styles that formed a ridiculous joke of a house. The owner had spent a small fortune designing, redesigning and furnishing the home in an attempt to convince his wife to move from New York to Louisiana for their retirement. It had taken one trip to Beauchamp for her to decide this wasn't the place for her. Fontenot's Folly had remained vacant ever since.

She'd assumed the home had fallen into disrepair in the decades since it had been built and was probably ready to be dozed by now. But as Bishop parked his black Dodge Charger in the circular driveway behind nearly a dozen other vehicles, the view through her passenger window proved all of her assumptions were completely wrong.

The main house was absolutely gorgeous and pristine. Although definitely a mishmash of styles, from French Colonial to creole cottage, it somehow managed to blend them perfectly. Traditional white clapboard siding was interspersed with floor-to-ceiling windows across a sweeping veranda that appeared to wrap around the entire first floor. White pillars held up the second floor gallery on the front of the house that boasted intricate wrought iron railings. Blush-colored brick stairs led to the solid glass double-front doors.

The acreage surrounding the home was just as stunning, dotted with century old oak trees dripping Spanish moss. But by far, what was most impressive about it was the gorgeous man who'd been leaning against one of the pillars when they'd driven up, and who was now heading toward her door.

Mason.

She got out of the car and turned to thank Bishop, but he was already shouting distance from the car, heading toward the backyard in the direction of some absolutely delicious-smelling food. Something spicy and familiar.

"Welcome to the Seeker's temporary headquarters."

She turned around, her heart speeding up just to be standing so close to him. "Mason. It's so good to see you."

"Same here. I've missed you. It's been, what, three days?"

"Four. Not that I'm counting."

He smiled. "Your father's doing better I heard?"

"Much. He's conscious and talking. No deficits from the head injury. He's in a regular room now, out of ICU. Still, even with him doing so well, it was hard to leave. But he insisted."

"He did?"

"He knows I want to help, to work on the investigation. He teased me that he was weary of me hovering around him, that he could rest much easier knowing I was here, with you and the Seekers. He basically kicked me out."

He moved closer, until their bodies were nearly touching. "I'm liking your father more and more."

"Mason?"

"Yes?"

"Would you please kiss me?"

His mouth curved in a sexy grin. Then he nearly brought her to her knees with one of those breath-stealing winks. "It would be my extreme pleasure."

He pulled her to him, one arm sliding around her back, the other cupping her head. And then he was kissing her the way she'd always wanted him to kiss her, since the first time Olivia had shared his picture and bragged about how honorable and wonderful he was. This kiss was nothing like the short, tame ones they'd shared before. This one was hot, wild. It shattered the memory of every kiss she'd ever had, searing her nerve endings and rocking her to her core.

When the kiss was over, she slumped back against the car to keep from falling down. He seemed just as shaken, bracing his hands on the roof on either side of her, struggling to catch his breath.

"Wow," she said, when she was able to talk again.

His shoulders shook with laughter. "Wow yourself, Hannah Cantrell. That was…there are no words."

"I have some. How about, where's that guesthouse where you said we'd stay?"

He groaned, then swore.

Her face heated with embarrassment. "Okay. Once again, not the reaction I was hoping for." She pushed his arm out of her way and started toward the main house.

"Oh, no you don't." He scooped her up in his arms and cradled her against his chest. "Don't be angry. I didn't swear because I *didn't* want to be with you. I swore because I *do*."

She hesitated, then looped her hands behind his head. "Then what's the problem?"

"The problem is that there's a catered crawfish-boil dinner-slash-party waiting for us behind the main house. Everyone's been working so hard that I felt some downtime for a few hours would benefit all of us. The entire team is here, minus Han, whose taking up guard duty at the hospital. And after the get-together, we're all going to review the status of the investigation. Our, ah, *tour* of the cottage will have to wait a bit longer. This has been planned since early this morning, long before I found out you'd be coming back to Beauchamp today. I'd cancel, but everyone's been looking forward to this."

"Oh goodness. I wouldn't dream of asking you to cancel. I'm sad to have to wait a little longer, but once again you're proving what an exceptional boss you are to think about your team like this. I think that's admirable, and sweet."

"Sweet enough to win me another kiss?" he teased.

"Definitely." She tightened her arms behind his neck and kissed him, pouring all her pent-up longing into every caress of her lips against his, every sweep of her tongue in an erotic duel as old as time.

The sound of laughter coming from the backyard had her pulling back to look over his shoulder. "Someone's having fun."

"Not as much fun as we're going to have once dinner and the meeting are over."

Her belly tightened. "Then we'd better hurry."

He grinned and set her down. They took off running.

In spite of her initial hope to hurry through the get-together and subsequent meeting so she could have some alone time with Mason, she couldn't remember laughing or enjoying herself this much in a long time. And she hadn't realized how keyed up and stressed she'd been until she'd begun to relax right along with Mason's team. He was a smart man to realize that his people needed some downtime, however brief. Hannah didn't think she'd have thought of it herself.

It had been hilarious seeing the looks on some of the Seekers' faces, particularly Dalton's, when Eli showed them how to eat mudbugs, or crawfish as most around here called them. When he broke off the tail and pulled out most of the meat, no one seemed to mind that. But when he sucked the shell and broke the claws to get every last piece from inside, Dalton turned green. He flat out refused to try them. At least until several of the others made fun of him. His face had turned red with indignation. Mimicking everything Eli had shown them, he managed to eat one of the Cajun delicacies. To his surprise, he'd loved it.

The sun had gone down long before they began gathering in a circle around a firepit, just a stone's throw from the bayou behind the main house. A seat by Mason seemed to miraculously open up when Hannah headed to the circle. It was obvious from the knowing looks and smiles that it wasn't a secret that she and Mason were interested in each other. Apparently gossip traveled just as fast among the Seekers as it did through Beauchamp.

When everyone fell silent, Mason started the meeting. "I hope you all had a good time tonight. Thanks, Eli, for helping extend a bit of Louisiana hospitality to everyone. I hear Dalton has such an affinity for the food that he just might move here when this is all over."

Dalton thumped his Stetson. "Yeah, right. Maybe after Eli ropes a calf and rides a bull with me in Montana, I'll consider it."

"You're on, cowboy." Eli grinned.

Dalton shook his head.

"I'd like to thank you all again too," Mason said, "for being willing to temporarily uproot your lives to come all this way and help me out. God willing, it will be over soon and we can all go home."

Hannah's smile dimmed at that. Mason glanced at her and she smiled as he continued his speech. But the smile was definitely forced. Just thinking about him leaving Beauchamp cast a heavy pall over the gathering for her.

Having been half in love with him for years, she'd been thrilled to finally meet him in person and confirm that he was every bit as wonderful as she'd expected. Then she'd become focused on helping him prove the charges against him were false. With everything that had happened, she hadn't stopped to think much beyond that, about what the future might hold for them. She'd figured that two people as attracted to each other as they were, well, that the pieces would fall into place for them. But as she thought about it now, she realized that was likely a fantasy, rather than reality.

Their outlooks on Beauchamp, and Sabine Parish, were polar opposites. Her family was here, her friends. The food, the culture, the music—everything about this place spoke to her heart. She couldn't imagine ever living anywhere else. And yet, the same wasn't true for Mason. He'd spent the last seven years hundreds of miles from here. He'd built a life, no doubt never expecting to return, not permanently anyway. Even if the charges were dropped against him, would that change how he felt about Beauchamp? How his family felt about him? Unlikely. How could there be a future between them with one of them in Louisiana and the other in Tennessee?

She twisted her hands together in her lap. Maybe staying in the cottage with him wasn't a good idea after all. Loving him, then losing him, would likely destroy her. Perhaps she should put the brakes on before it was too late for her heart to survive, if it wasn't already too late.

"Are you sure, Bryson? My brother? Wyatt?" Mason said.

Hannah blinked in confusion, realizing she'd missed whatever they'd been talking about.

Bryson nodded. "There are quite a few people on the list of Audrey's known associates that the local PI gave me. We're all having problems getting the locals to open up to us, but he's well-known around here and seems plugged in to the gossip scene. I have no reason to doubt that list. But when I saw Wyatt's name on there, it set off a few red flags. So we're digging deeper to determine his exact relationship with her."

"Wyatt didn't mention any kind of relationship with Audrey when we spoke. Let me know what else you find out."

"There's something else." He glanced at Brielle, who nodded.

Mason frowned. "What?"

Brielle, a former Gatlinburg police officer, spoke up. "You might be surprised to hear this, Mason, but Kira and I have been looking into the original case against your brother, Landon. The coincidences between that case and yours are too blatant to ignore. They could be related."

"Agreed. I've wondered myself whether the same killer was responsible for both murders. What's that got to do with what Bryson said about my brother?"

She motioned to Bryson.

He sighed. "After seeing his name on that list, and knowing the similarities between the current case and the old one, I dug into Wyatt's finances."

Mason stared at him a long moment. "He's a financial advisor. Runs his own business. He's always done really well, from what I could tell."

"Well, actually, that's the problem. He hasn't always done well. It's not obvious at first glance. But you know our resources, our experience as a team, following the money. As near as I can see, your brother's business has never been a particularly thriving enterprise. He doesn't even have that many clients. And yet, he has an expensive home, car, a very comfortable lifestyle. Unless you're giving him money, I can't explain it."

"I'm not. I've offered money to all of my family. Wyatt refused."

Bryson nodded. "Well, his rise in fortunes seems to have begun about two years before your older brother was framed for Ms. DuBois's murder."

Mason grew still. "Two years?"

Bryson nodded.

Hannah glanced back and forth between them. "Is that significant?"

Mason didn't say anything.

Bryson looked at her and said, "When Mason brought the FBI into town to investigate corruption, they found it had basically begun two years earlier, when the mayor started his little crime syndicate."

"Wait. You're not saying his brother was…" She pressed her hand to her mouth.

Mason glanced at her. "He's insinuating that Wyatt was as corrupt as the others, way back when, and that he worked with the mayor to line his own pockets. Aren't you, Bryson?"

"I'm still in the early stages of the research. I could be completely wrong. Look, I'm sorry. I shouldn't have even brought it up. I'll go back and—"

"Stop." Mason scrubbed his face with his hands, then looked at all of them before speaking. "We're a team. We're in this together. And you all know I've been trying to solve my oldest brother's murder for years. If solving it takes you into uncomfortable territory for me, so be it. If Wyatt was involved in the corruption and didn't get caught in the FBI net, then I want to know about it. I can't figure out how that involves Audrey, and rather doubt that it does. But I'm not going to ask you to not follow every lead wherever it takes you." He nodded at Bryson. "I appreciate that you're doing as thorough a job as you can. Please keep doing it."

Bryson nodded but didn't look happy about it.

Brielle squeezed his shoulder, then cleared her throat. "Kira, Bryson and I have all been working on looking into Landon's frame-up because of its similarities to yours. And I was wondering if you could give us a quick history lesson about what happened. Maybe that will help. We know the basics—that your brother was found standing over his live-in girlfriend's body at their home, and she'd been shot to death. But aside from reading the case file, we don't have much else. Is there anything you can add around that, to frame it for us?"

Hannah perked up. She'd like to know more about what had happened too. It wasn't one of those subjects that Olivia talked about. And not something others around town brought up in daily conversation.

"Well, to *frame it*, I'll quote former Louisiana representative Billy Tauzin who once said that 'half of Louisiana is under water and the other half is under indictment.' Unfortunately, that's not too far off. The state has a history of corrupt politicians from the governor's mansion on down, and Beauchamp is no exception. When I was asked by the mayor to be the next chief of police, my ego was big enough to think he'd asked me because he saw my amazing potential, even though I hadn't been a police officer long enough to typically be considered for that kind of position. I learned the hard way that the real reason he asked me was *because* of my inexperience. He assumed I either wouldn't notice the corruption, or I'd ignore it."

Hannah put her hand on top of his arm. "He was wrong on both counts, wasn't he?"

"He was. But not right away. In the beginning I was full of myself, blinded by the shiny gold eagles on my uniform. I looked up to the mayor. I was so impressed by his professionalism and willingness to help people that I got Olivia a job working for him as an intern while still in high school so she could put that on her college applications. Once I realized what a snake he was, I asked her to quit. She refused, as any typical rebellious teenager would. So I pulled out the big guns to force her to quit."

Brielle grinned. "You told your parents?"

He smiled. "I did. I didn't have proof yet about his illegal activities, but I'd seen and heard enough to know something was seriously wrong. My parents called the mayor and told them their minor child—she was fifteen at the time—no longer had their permission to work there. He had no choice but to let her go after that. She resented me for a long time."

"She doesn't anymore," Hannah said. "She practically worships you."

He held his hands out in a helpless gesture. "She seems to. But I've never felt I deserved that. I think she's so devastated over Landon's death that she clings to her two remaining brothers."

"What happened to the mayor?" Brielle asked.

"He killed himself at home one night. That was after Landon's case was adjudicated, and his death. The mayor was going to be arrested soon. He must have realized that and took the easy way out. He left a wife and two small kids. His death left a huge gap in the FBI's investigation. Many of the answers to their questions went to the grave with him. It was apparent that he was involved in the framing of my brother for Mandy DuBois's murder. But we never found out why he did it, and who the real killer was. His suicide was a lose-lose for everyone involved. But there was one thing that came out that made me glad I'd forced Olivia to quit working for him. Some of his interns came out saying he'd made inappropriate advances toward them. I asked Olivia if he'd ever tried anything. Thankfully he hadn't. She got out in time to not become one of his victims." He shook his head in disgust.

Hannah pressed a hand to her heart, hating that anyone had been preyed upon by the mayor. She'd never heard that before. She was so glad that Mason had pressured Olivia's parents to have her quit working for him.

Jaxon sat forward in his chair, hands clasped with his arms resting on his knees. "You said you proved Landon didn't do it. How did you prove that without finding out who the real killer was?"

"Actually, it's something you'd appreciate, Jaxon. You're the video whiz kid around here. It was a video that proved he was innocent. I was able to show he had an alibi for the moment that Mandy DuBois was shot. Unfortunately, too late to save him. After his conviction, I started over from the very beginning, trying to find out what was missed. When I canvassed the neighborhood where Landon and Mandy lived, I spoke to his neighbor across the street. Turns out, one of his surveillance cameras had a perfect angle of Landon's second floor. It clearly showed all the lights were out upstairs. Then you hear a gunshot. The light goes on and Landon jumps out of bed and runs through the bedroom doorway. Seconds later, he's back, grabbing his phone and calling 911 before running back downstairs. There was only one shot fired that night and it was clearly fired *before* Landon went downstairs. Mandy's body was on the first floor, in the main living area."

Jaxon frowned. "But if the video provided an alibi, how was he convicted?"

Hannah threaded her fingers through his, sensing Mason's pain as he relayed the story. He let out a deep breath and squeezed her hand.

"The video was never presented at the trial. The only way I got a copy was because the neighbor, who'd given the video to the police, had kept a copy on his computer. He said when he heard that Landon was convicted, he was surprised. What he hadn't known was that the video was destroyed and the defense never knew it existed. If that neighbor hadn't saved a copy, to this day we wouldn't have proof that Landon was innocent. That video is what clued me in that there were some in my own police force who were crooked, concealing evidence in the case. It was also pivotal in me winning the civil suit against the town."

"Was there other key evidence that helped you win the lawsuit?" This time it was Dalton who asked the question.

"Gunshot residue. The video clearly showed what clothes my brother was wearing that night—a white T-shirt and blue boxers. His T-shirt didn't have a pocket on it. At trial, the prosecutor presented a white T-shirt and blue boxers as the outfit Landon wore that night. But the T-shirt had a pocket. Landon had several T-shirts and boxers that were similar and didn't realize they'd switched the clothing. The outfit presented in court was GSR positive, supposedly proving he'd fired a gun. But since the shirt wasn't his, it was obvious someone put gunshot residue on another shirt they switched out, to make him seem guilty. Losing the video could have been argued away as an innocent mistake that someone totally forgot about. Switching his clothes was proof positive of evidence tampering."

"Geesh." Dalton shook his head. "And these are the people with your fate in their hands right now."

"Yeah, well. Most of those people are in prison. But, yes, it's scary to think that a similar setup is in the works again. And I don't know who's behind it. There were several other things my lawyers and I presented at the civil trial. But the most significant in my mind was that our crime scene reconstruction specialist proved Mandy was shot from about fifteen feet away. Based on the angle of the body in the crime scene photos, her killer was standing in the kitchen. But the police

found Landon standing right over her, which is incon-
sistent. It's just one more thing that casts doubt on the
crime scene."

"What about the murder weapon?" Hannah asked.
Her face heated and she looked around the circle. "I'm
sorry. I'm not part of your team. I shouldn't be asking
questions."

Mason very deliberately lifted their joined hands and
kissed her knuckles, with everyone watching. "You're
on *my* team, Hannah. You can ask any questions you
want."

She gave him a grateful smile, but silently berated
herself for interrupting.

"The gun was Landon's. He identified it during the
trial. It was a Sig Sauer 9mm. He got it as a present, all
of us brothers did, from my dad when we each turned
twenty-one. Landon kept it downstairs, in an end table
drawer. One theory is that an intruder, a would-be burglar, found the gun, then hid in the pantry when Mandy
and Landon came home. After Landon went to bed,
maybe Mandy heard something or saw him sneaking
out and he shot her, then quickly wiped the gun and
tossed it down beside her before running out the back
door."

Bishop gestured to him, taking a turn at asking a
question. "Regardless of who the shooter was, why
would the police falsify evidence to frame your brother?
Why go to all that trouble?"

"I've asked myself that same question many times.
There are two answers that seem plausible. One is that
the burglar theory is accurate and the police who framed

Landon did it either to get back at me because of the on-going FBI investigation, or to distract both me and the agent who was looking into the corruption."

Bishop nodded. "Makes sense. What's the second theory?"

"There was no burglary. Mandy was the intended target and the plan all along was to frame Landon so the real killer wouldn't take the fall." He shrugged. "That one is pretty thin. I've never found anyone who wanted to harm Mandy. I've got no evidence to back that up."

"But your gut is telling you that's what happened, isn't it?" Bishop asked.

Mason slowly nodded. "It is. I've always felt that someone came there with the intent to kill Mandy."

Everyone fell silent, as if they were all reflecting back on that fateful night and trying to fit the pieces together.

"Mason?" Brielle asked. "There's one additional piece of evidence you haven't mentioned that has been bothering me since I began looking into this. Mandy DuBois's clothes, what she was wearing the night of the shooting."

He frowned. "What about them?"

"She was still clinging to life when your brother found her. They cut her clothes off at the hospital. The outfit was bagged and tagged and kept all these years with the rest of the evidence. It's still there. I saw it yesterday at the police station, when they let me review everything in a conference room. Given what you've said about other evidence being falsified or hidden or thrown out, I figure that no one considered her clothing to be of any evidentiary value or it might have gone missing. If you're okay with it, I'd like to take her clothes to a private lab to have them perform extensive DNA testing of the bloodstains."

"A private lab, because our state lab is backed up for months?" he asked.

"Exactly. Plus, they're neutral in this. We could get results in days if you're willing to throw enough money at it. Maybe even hours. It's not the testing itself that takes long anymore. It's the requests queued up, and lack of funding."

"I don't mind the testing and I'll certainly pay for it. But if the shooter was fifteen feet away when he pulled the trigger, it's not like his DNA will be on her clothes."

"Agreed. But going along with your theory that someone came there to kill her, maybe they talked to her first. Maybe they got close up, touched her clothes, got their sweat on them. He could have backed away before firing so he wouldn't get blood on him. I know it sounds crazy and is probably a huge waste of resources. But I'd like to at least give it a try. Who knows. Maybe it will lead us to the killer."

"Okay. Do it. If the police fight you on it, talk to our resident FBI agent. Holland should be able to convince them to sign the evidence over to the lab for testing."

"Will do. Thanks."

"Thank *you*."

Dalton thumped his Stetson, getting everyone's attention. "If we're through talking about your brother's case, I'd like to talk about yours. Bryson shared the PI's report on Audrey Broussard with me, and I feel like there are a lot of gaps in the timeline leading up to her death that someone who knows her might be able to fill in. Beauchamp PD has been cooperative and provided me the address of her parents. Her being an only child, that's pretty much the only family she has here in town. But I didn't want to talk to them without asking you first. Are you okay with that?"

"No. I'm not." Mason sighed and scrubbed his face again. "Sorry, Dalton. I know you're trying to help. But when nearly everyone else in this town turned their backs on me, including Audrey, her parents were about the only ones who didn't. They suffered a lot of fallout for publicly supporting me during the civil trial and all the hate that was directed at me because of it. I can't even imagine the pain they're feeling right now. And I don't want to be responsible for causing more. That's the only reason I haven't contacted them myself with my condolences. I'd like to help them in any way that I can. But given that I'm the only suspect in their daughter's murder, it's beyond inappropriate for me to go near them. And I don't want anyone on my team imposing on them either."

"Understood. I'll work with Bryson on the timeline without bothering the Broussards."

"Thanks, Dalton." He looked around the circle. "I know more of you have updates on the things you're investigating. But it's getting late and I don't want to keep you any longer. Let's regroup tomorrow morning and finish the meeting before everyone heads into town. I've got a local café dropping off breakfast here at nine. It'll be set up in the dining room. Get a plate and we'll meet in the gathering room, since that's the only place inside big enough to hold all of us comfortably. Sound good?"

There was a chorus of agreement and the Seekers began drifting up to the main house in groups of twos and threes. When it was just Mason and Hannah left, he gently pulled her to her feet.

Her belly jumped with a mixture of longing and dread. Then she met his gaze, and realized she wasn't the only one with reservations. His expression was serious, with none of the teasing or heat from earlier.

"What's wrong?" she whispered.

"We need to talk."

Chapter Sixteen

Hannah's purse and small suitcase were sitting by the front door inside the cottage. Bishop must have put them here for her at some point during the evening. She'd completely forgotten to get them out of his car.

The cottage was cozy yet luxurious—from the modern bright white kitchenette in one corner to the cushy-looking white leather sectional in the center of the room. The bedroom door stood open, revealing a four-poster king-size bed with frothy white curtains and a down comforter, just waiting to wrap someone in its embrace. And not far from where she and Mason stood just inside the cottage, a silver serving tray sat on a decorative table, holding a bottle of champagne in a bucket of ice. Two champagne flutes sat beside it waiting for a loving couple to enjoy them.

A single tear slid down her cheek. Everything was perfect. And yet, it wasn't.

Mason stepped behind her and gently pulled her back against him, his hands caressing her shoulders. "That mirror over the fireplace tells me my fears were well-founded. That's not a tear of joy sliding down your beautiful face."

She drew a shaky breath and wiped her eyes before turning around. "I think we've both come to some kind of realization tonight, thus the tears. You first. You said you wanted to talk."

"The look on your face at the meeting tonight was full of regret and worry. The later it got, the more worried you looked. It dawned on me that you were probably starting to dread agreeing to go to the cottage with me. I've been pushing you too hard, too fast. You're not ready for this step, and I never should have expected you to be. Not with everything else going on."

She frowned. "What? No. No, that's not it at all."

It was his turn to frown. "Then…you still want us to stay here? You want to make love with me?"

"More than anything."

A look of relief crossed his face. "Then my radar is really out of whack. I thought you were having second thoughts." He reached for her, but she quickly stepped back. He slowly lowered his arms. "Okay. Now I'm really confused."

She let out a shuddering breath. "I'd like nothing better than to lock us both in here for a week without coming up for air."

"And that's a bad thing?"

"It is," she whispered brokenly. "It's bad because, for you, it would be a pleasant interlude between two consenting adults who *really* like each other. But for me, it would be the culmination of years of longing, of building you up in my mind until—"

"Ah. I understand. Olivia built me up so much that reality doesn't hold a candle to the fantasy." He smiled sadly. "It's okay. My ego can handle the rejection. It might take a while, but I'll move on. Eventually. Stay here as long as you want. Come up to the main house during the day and brainstorm the case, if you'd like. We can just be friends. Somehow." He winked, but it didn't have the heat or the sexy charm his winks usually had. "You're safe here. We have perimeter cameras that will sound an alarm if anyone comes within a mile of this place. I can stay in the main house. No hard feelings." He started to turn away.

"Mason, wait." She grabbed his arm. "I wasn't finished. You have it backward. Reality *eclipses* the fantasy. You are more than I ever dreamed you could be. And I'm not just talking about how ridiculously gorgeous you are."

His eyes widened, but she hurried to explain before he said anything else. "It's what's inside your heart, your mind, your soul that are so amazing. Don't you see? I'm falling for you. The real you, not the Olivia hero worship you. And if we make love, I'm afraid my heart will tumble over the edge and I'll fall completely in love with you."

"Hannah, I—"

She pressed her fingers against his mouth, stopping him. "We can't make love, Mason. I have to protect my heart, while I still can. Unless you can tell me that you plan on moving back to Beauchamp after your name is cleared and you're a free man. Can you do that? Promise me you'd be okay moving here if we fall for each other? That you could see a future for yourself in this town? With me?"

He stared at her a long moment, before slowly shaking his head. "No. I can't see a future for me in Beauchamp, or even in Louisiana. But I could live anywhere else, if I was with someone I loved. Do I see forever when I look at you? Honestly, I'm not sure yet. Everything's happened so fast. But the *idea* of forever, with you, doesn't scare me. And that's saying something. Since breaking up with Audrey years ago, I've never, ever, felt the way I feel when I'm with you. Why not just enjoy the moment, our time together, and see where it leads? If it leads to forever, then we can move anywhere you want. We can figure out all of that later."

"No. We can't. After nearly losing my father this week and seeing my mother beaten down, so in need of the love and support of her family, there's no way I could leave them. And I know they could never leave Sabine Parish. They were born here in Beauchamp and moved to Many right after high school, then returned a few years ago so dad could be chief. Their parents grew up here. So did their parents, and their grandparents and theirs. My roots are here, deep roots. I have no choice but to stay. And it's a choice I gladly make. Where you look around and see corruption and the evil of the past, I see my hometown, lifelong friends and a loving family. Knowing I could never leave, and that you could never stay, it's pointless to explore this relationship any further. All it would do is break my heart. It broke once, when I lost my husband, and it took years for me to recover." She looked up into his tormented gaze, her tears flowing freely now. "If I *had* you, if I loved you with all my heart, then lost you, it would wreck me."

He stared down at her, his expression unreadable. Finally, he smiled. "My offer to stay, to help in the investigation, still stands. I hope to see you at the main house, that you won't feel awkward and not want to join the rest of us. We'll get through this." He took her hand in his and pressed a whisper-soft kiss against her knuckles. Then he left her.

Chapter Seventeen

Going to the main house the next morning was probably a mistake, but Hannah couldn't pretend she didn't care about the investigation. She wanted to know who'd shot her dad. And she wanted to know who'd killed Audrey and was trying to frame Mason. Even if there was no future for her and Mason as a couple, she cared deeply for him. And she wanted to support him in any way that she could. Maybe, even with all those smart Seekers digging up clues, she'd still be able to spot something they didn't. As long as there was even a slight chance that she might help in some way, she'd risk the awkward reception she might get from Mason—and the others once they realized their relationship had changed.

Everyone was already assembled in the cavernous main room when she arrived. Since they were taking turns giving summaries about their individual work on the case, as they had around the firepit last night, she quietly made her way across the room to an empty chair. But when she sat, Mason, who was several places away on a love seat, motioned to Dalton sitting beside him. Dalton moved to another seat, and Mason looked at her, clearly an invitation for her to join him. Relief flashed through her and she quickly crossed to him, returning his smile with one of her own. Things weren't the way she wanted them to be between them. But at least he wasn't treating her like a stranger.

Bryson was talking about some kind of financial reports on various people who'd been seen with Audrey in the weeks prior to her death. Hannah tuned him out for a while, but as she looked around at the Seekers, she realized that one of them was missing. She leaned close to Mason and whispered, "Where's Brielle?"

"She's in New Orleans at a private lab, getting Mandy DuBois's clothing tested."

She nodded and tried to pay attention to Bryson, but finances didn't interest her in the least. What she wanted to know was whether they'd figured out some good suspects. Still, when he said the name Wyatt Ford, it definitely got her attention. She remembered Bryson had mentioned Wyatt's finances, and that his company was having problems. He'd even mentioned he might be associated with the old mayor in some way. Had he found out something concrete?

Mason was riveted on what Bryson was saying. Hannah listened as carefully as she could, hoping whatever Bryson had found out didn't implicate Wyatt in Mandy's murder. Because that's where this seemed to be headed. And something that awful—that one brother could frame another for murder—wasn't something she'd wish on her worst enemy. Mason had suffered enough in his life already. Surely the Fates wouldn't add something like that as an additional burden on his shoulders. Because, after all, if Wyatt had framed Landon, what was to stop him from framing Mason eight years later?

Bryson cleared his throat. "I know it's a lot to take in. I still have a long way to go to get it nailed down. It's taking forever to weed through the mayor's finances and Wyatt's. But it doesn't look good. There are withdrawals of large sums from the mayor's accounts that seem to match deposits to Wyatt's a few days later. And yet, the mayor doesn't appear on any list of clients of Wyatt's financial advisor company. I've turned the information over to Special Agent Holland to see if he can dig deeper. I've gone as far as I can without crossing a line." He arched his brows at Mason as if in question.

Mason shook his head. "Let Holland work that angle. I don't see an urgent need right now to take more risks on our end. The last thing I want to do in Beauchamp is break any laws, no matter how tempting. Let's keep it legal."

Hannah blinked in surprise. She'd understood that Mason's company might bend a law now and then to protect a client, maybe even break one if it was a matter of life or death. But Mason's future, his life, was at risk here. She'd have expected him to be okay with pushing the limits. But as usual, he put everyone but himself first and apparently didn't think his own situation was worth the trade-off of putting some of his own people in a tenuous situation. She admired him for that. But it also bothered her that he might not be putting every resource he had into his own defense.

"I'm willing," Bryson assured him. "If you change your mind, let me know."

"Thanks, Bryson." Mason scanned the room. "I know we've found ties between Wyatt and Audrey." He cleared his throat. "Has anyone found any ties between Wyatt and Mandy DuBois, Landon's girlfriend who was murdered?"

Everyone exchanged glances but no one offered any information.

"All right," Mason said, sounding relieved. "I believe Jaxon was next. Hannah, you'll want to hear this. He gave me a preview earlier this morning."

Jaxon, a former marine MP, stood to give his summary, probably a formality he'd learned from the military, because most of the Seekers were more laid-back. But as he began, Hannah was more interested in Mason.

"Are you okay?" she whispered.

"Because of Wyatt?"

"Yes."

He leaned close to her ear. "I know it looks bad. But things looked bad for Landon, and for me too. And neither of us were killers. For all I know, someone else is behind both frame-ups and is purposely lining up Wyatt to take the fall when things go bad. Maybe someone has a vendetta against our family and is going after all three brothers. I'm trying to not let emotions cloud my judgment. But I'm also giving him the benefit of the doubt. I'd never want to accuse someone of something they didn't do. It's a miserable feeling."

"You're an amazing man, Mason Ford," she whispered.

He stared at her so long, her face heated. But she couldn't read his expression well enough to know what he was thinking. It bothered her, because she'd always been able to read him before now.

Jaxon said something about videos in her neighborhood, which had both her and Mason paying attention again. He told them about various knock-and-talks he'd done, going door-to-door trying to find anyone who might have snapped a picture out a window or had a doorbell surveillance system that might have caught a car driving by or the shooting itself.

"What it boils down to," he said, "is a mountain of video in that part of the city. And it paid off. I was able to point Beauchamp PD to two specific recordings that were high quality and left no doubt about who shot Chief Landry." He looked directly at Hannah. "Abrams and Donnelly were in the car together. Abrams was driving. Donnelly shot your father."

She started trembling, even though it was basically what she'd expected. "Th…thank you, Jaxon."

"Yes, ma'am."

Mason put his arm around her shoulders and she gratefully leaned into his side.

A loud knock sounded on the door.

Bryson, who was the closest to the entrance, disappeared into the foyer. A moment later, he led Chief Murphy into the room.

Murphy seemed surprised as he looked around. "I didn't expect this big of an audience. Mason, Hannah, I've got some developments to speak to you about. Am I talking to everyone or just you two?"

Mason crossed to him and shook hands. "We have no secrets here. Everyone stays."

"Very well."

Mason sat beside Hannah. One of the Seekers got up from a nearby chair and offered it to Murphy so he could be closer to them. He nodded his thanks and sat.

"First, Hannah, has anyone updated you on what the Seekers found out last night?"

"That your deputies shot my father?"

He winced. "Yes. I wanted to let you know they've been caught. They'd holed up at an old fishing cabin on Donnelly's uncle's property. We found them before sunup this morning. Al's been interviewing them and the DA made a deal—if they came clean about who was with them in Gatlinburg, and why, he wouldn't seek the death penalty for them trying to kill your father. And before you get mad about that, your father gave his consent to the deal an hour ago."

Mason took her hand, helping to calm her immediate outrage. She threaded her fingers in his and let him take the lead.

"What was their explanation, Chief? Who hired them?"

"Audrey did. Actually, she hired our notorious two former deputies, and they brought in three more guys. Under oath, knowing if we catch them in a lie the death penalty is back on the table, they swore that Audrey hired them as her backup plan to kidnap you if you turned her down in Gatlinburg. Her idea was to, ah, seduce you and convince you to stay with her. She felt that if you woke up in Beauchamp, you'd be inclined to spend time with her and work things out."

Mason frowned. "That's bizarre. And even if it's

true, why would Abrams or Donnelly, or one of their thugs, kill her and then frame me?"

"I'm getting to that part. But before I do, I want to speak to the autopsy results. Mason, Audrey had glioblastoma, stage 4."

He stared at him in shock. "Brain cancer?"

"Yes. The medical examiner called around and discovered that she'd been getting treatment in Lafayette at Our Lady of Lourdes JD Moncus Cancer Center. The date of her diagnosis was right around the time she bought that SUV—something that Al, Detective Latimer, was able to validate. My guess is that she didn't want people seeing her red convertible in Lafayette and asking questions. She kept her illness to herself, didn't even tell her parents. It might have been because she didn't want anyone pitying her. Or maybe she didn't want people hearing about her illness and not hiring her for decorating jobs. The ME says her cognitive skills would have definitely been impaired. At her last treatment, her doctor told her next time she needed to come back with someone else driving her or he'd officially work with the state to take away her license. She missed her next appointment and didn't answer their calls."

Mason's hand tightened on Hannah's. "She was pale and tired-looking in Gatlinburg." His voice was quiet and strained. "I asked if she felt okay and she insisted that she did."

"You didn't know," Hannah told him. "She didn't want you to know."

Murphy rested his forearms on his knees. "I think

you can feel better knowing she wasn't in her right mind when she arranged your abduction."

He stared at Murphy. "If what you're saying is true, how did she end up shot to death and me framed for it?"

"The blood spatter evidence shows a void in front of Audrey."

"The killer was standing in front of her, close to her, when he shot her."

"Someone was standing in front of her, yes. The evidence shows they were about four feet away. There were gunpowder burns beneath her chin, where the barrel was pressed against her skin. Blood sprayed back into the barrel. Gunshot residue was on her hands, her clothes and the floor right beneath her. There's also a scrape mark in the blood, showing after the shooting the gun was picked up from the floor. When you picked up the gun in the bedroom upstairs, there wasn't any blood on the outside or we'd have found blood in the bedroom, or even on your hands. There also weren't any prints on the gun and no GSR. There wasn't any gunshot residue on you either."

Mason gave him a hard look. "Murphy, are you trying to tell me that Audrey killed herself? And that someone else wiped the gun and tried to frame me as if it was murder?"

"That's exactly what I'm saying."

"You're wrong. She wouldn't do that."

Hannah touched his forearm. "I don't think he's finished. Let's hear him out, okay?"

His tortured gaze met hers, and he gave her a crisp nod before looking back at the acting chief.

Murphy smiled at Hannah and continued. "What we don't know yet is who framed you. Donnelly and Abrams swear they had nothing to do with that. They said they responded to the anonymous 911 call and were shocked to find Audrey dead and you standing over her. Rather than do the right thing and admit that they'd been part of the crew who kidnapped you and had brought you there—which likely would have kept you from serious consideration as a suspect—they remained silent, so they wouldn't get in trouble."

Murphy shook his head in disgust. "Other than you holding the gun, there is zero evidence to show you did this. None of the forensics point to you. There'd be no reason for you to clean the gun and then be found with it. If you shot her, you'd have run right then, not risked being found in the house. And the evidence shows whoever was there when she shot herself was standing too far away to have held the gun under her chin. No matter how you look at it, there's just no way that you shot her. Whoever was there watched her shoot herself, and for some reason thought to frame you for it after the fact. They likely called 911 as part of that. We'll work hard to figure out who that is."

He stood and pulled a gun from his pocket. Reversing directions, he held it handle first toward Mason. "The DA said it was okay to give you back your weapon."

Mason didn't take the gun. "I'm out on bail. I'm not allowed to have a firearm."

"The DA has dropped all charges against you. Mason Ford, you're a free man."

Chapter Eighteen

Hannah saw Chief Murphy out and thanked him. But when she went back into the main room, there was no sign of Mason. Many of the Seekers had left for other parts of the house. Others sat around the expansive room, working on laptops or talking on their phones.

Dalton caught her attention from across the room and motioned toward the wall of glass that looked out over the bayou. Mason was standing on the dock in one of his gray suits, his hands in his pockets, staring out at the cypress and tupelo trees. Yesterday morning, she wouldn't have hesitated to check on him. This morning, she didn't know if he'd want her there.

She started to sit, but the serious, quiet and somewhat intimidating Bishop crossed to her.

"He doesn't want any of us with him right now," he told her.

She nodded. "I figured. He wants to be alone. Because of Audrey. Finding out she killed herself has to be a huge blow, regardless of the state of their relationship when she died."

"You seem to know him really well, in spite of only meeting him a relatively short time ago."

Her face heated. "Yes, well. I've kind of hero-worshipped him from afar for a long time. His baby sister, Olivia, is a good friend and talks about him. A lot." She cleared her throat. "And now I'm talking way too much. Since he doesn't want anyone to bother him, I'll just sit and wait."

"You misunderstood me. He doesn't want *us* out there, the Seekers. But I'm quite certain he'd want *you*. He'd never ask. But if you're inclined to join him, even if you don't say anything, it could make a difference."

Impossibly, her face heated even more. "I don't think so. Last night, well, he won't want to see me. Honestly, I probably should just go home." She started to turn away but he moved to block her.

"Ms. Cantrell. I found him in the library this morning, asleep on the couch. So I already knew something had gone wrong between you two. But he still cares about you, very much. And as his best friend, whose known him for many years, I'm certain that he needs you."

He needs you. She looked toward the wall of glass, at the lone figure on the dock, and had to blink back the threat of tears. "Thank you, Bishop."

Without a word, he walked away.

She paused by a mirror on one wall and checked her makeup, then fussed with her hair, before realizing a couple of the Seekers were smiling at her primping. She squared her shoulders, then headed outside, praying she wasn't making a mistake. The last thing she wanted was to hurt him, or make things worse.

When she reached the dock, she made no effort to soften her footfalls. She didn't want to surprise him, and wanted him to have the opportunity to tell her to go away.

He didn't.

Instead, as soon as she stopped beside him, he pulled her against his chest.

A pent-up breath shuddered out of her, and she slid her arms around his waist, holding on tight, telling him with actions, if not words, that she cared about him, that she would do anything in her power to take away his pain.

It felt so good to be held by him, to feel the tension slowly easing from his body. Maybe Bishop was right and she was helping after all. He kissed the top of her head. But instead of letting go, he took her hand in his and faced the bayou again.

"I'm so sorry about Audrey," she whispered. "I can't imagine your pain."

He squeezed her hand. "It hurts more than I expected. But I think what hurts the most is that people will remember the wrong things about her, that she orchestrated my kidnapping and fired the gun that killed her. That's not who she was."

"It's was her illness, the brain tumor. People who matter will realize that and remember her kindly."

"You're a good person, Hannah Cantrell. Having you here helps. Thank you."

This time, it was her turn to squeeze his hand.

They stood a long time, watching the Spanish moss dip and sway in the slightly cool breeze. A giant white egret landed in the top of one of the cypress trees. Insects buzzed and flitted from lily pad to lily pad, while somewhere in the distance a bullfrog croaked.

"I can't make sense of it." His deep voice broke the silence.

She let go of his hand and turned to face him. "Tell me."

He glanced over at her. "Audrey was a fighter. It was something I admired about her, how strong she was, and driven. I keep thinking about her being told she had terminal cancer and imagining her reaction. And I just can't see her giving up."

"The suicide."

He winced, then nodded.

"The tumor—"

"Doesn't matter. I'm telling you, if ten doctors told her she was terminal, she'd find an eleventh doctor who said there was hope. She would have fought to the very end for every second she had left, for every breath in her body. She wanted to live. Even if the tumor was affecting her judgment, her self-preservation instinct would have kicked in. I can't see any way that she'd have killed herself. Period."

"Okay. If anyone would know, you would. So the alternative is—"

"Someone murdered her and made it look like a suicide." He put his hands on her shoulders. "I know what I said sounds outlandish. But I also know something else—how crooked and underhanded some of the people in this town have been in the past. Like Abrams and Donnelly. Trusted public servants who were basically thugs for hire. What if someone wanted Audrey's murder to look like a suicide?"

"Why would they? What do they stand to gain?"

He let her go and raked a hand through his short, dark hair. "I don't know. I feel like I'm back where it all started, drowning in questions without enough answers."

"Let's talk it through," she said. "Does anyone benefit financially from her death?"

"No. My guys did a full financial investigation on her. She barely had enough life insurance for her burial. She made a good living, and she had investments that helped her keep a good lifestyle. But her assets weren't enough to tantalize someone into killing her. Not in my opinion."

"Okay, revenge?"

Again he shook his head. "She could be abrasive, but never mean. I can't imagine her doing anything that would make someone resent her enough to go after her like that."

"Love? People kill the ones they love all the time. It's a powerful emotion and can make people do things they wouldn't normally do."

"I don't think so."

"Well, that only leaves one other motive that I can think of. Someone wanted her quiet. She knew something, and they didn't want anyone else to find out about it."

He cocked his head, studying her. "You're not trying to talk sense into me and tell me it's a suicide."

"Why would I? You knew her better than anyone. And I'm right with you on the corruption around here, or incompetency. Maybe both. If you think someone killed her, then I'm 100 percent behind you on that. Even if she pulled the trigger, someone forced her to do it. Somehow."

He slowly shook his head. "You're amazing. Thank you."

She slid her arm around him and gave him a quick hug before stepping back.

"All right," he said. "I'll call Chief Murphy and tell him my suspicions. I'll ask him to order another autopsy, have the crime scene techs go over the scene again. Look at everything with a fresh perspective. They've missed something, an important piece of information that will prove it wasn't a suicide."

"Don't you think calling Murphy is risky? What if he tries to pin her murder on you again?"

"With everything else he said about the scene, I don't think he will." He took his gun out, studying it. "Someone used my gun to kill her. It's still so hard to believe." He idly turned it upside down and ran his fingers over two deep parallel lines cut into the bottom of the grip.

"What are those?" she asked. "I've never seen a gun with grooves like that."

"My dad's a retired machinist and a big proponent of concealed carry for self-defense. He taught all of us about gun safety. Remember earlier I said he gave us each a gun on our twenty-first birthdays? My sisters picked out different types. But us guys all wanted the same kind. To tell them apart, my dad machined those grooves onto the bottom of each gun, corresponding to each son's birth order."

"Ah. One for Landon, two for you, three for Wyatt?"

"You got it. If any of us are carrying when we go to visit him, he makes us put our guns in a special box on a table in the foyer. Or, at least, he did, back when we all were in Beauchamp. When we left, we'd check the grooves, make sure we took the right gun." He ran his thumb across the grooves, a half smile curving his lips. "I'd forgotten about that."

"Good memories?"

"Good memories. There was always some kind of tension in our house, but overall it was a good place to grow up. It's only after what happened to Landon that it all went to hell." He holstered his gun, then pulled out his phone and frowned at the screen.

"Something wrong?" she asked.

"Olivia's been texting me but I didn't realize it. She's at my parents' house. Apparently she's finally heard about me being charged, then let go and doesn't understand what's going on. She asked if I'd come over and explain everything. My parents said it was okay."

"Okay for you to come over? They should be *begging* you to come over. Or better yet, they should have been at the police station day one demanding answers and trying to help you."

"You don't understand the hell they went through when the town turned against all of us. They don't want to go through that again. I'm surprised they'd even risk me being seen going over there."

Hannah was careful to keep the anger from her voice when she spoke again. "Are you going?"

"I don't see a reason not to. I'd like to see Olivia, make sure she's okay. Calm her fears." He sent a quick text before putting his phone away. "I can call Murphy on the way there and discuss Audrey." He cleared his throat, suddenly seeming unsure of himself. "Do you want me to drop you off at your house? I had your SUV moved there, so you won't be stranded. With Abrams and Donnelly captured, you should be safe."

"Actually, if you don't mind, I'd like to go with you to your parents' house. As your…friend, I want to be there for you." She put her hand on his arm. "Please."

He smiled. "My very special friend. I'd like that. Let's go."

Chapter Nineteen

Mason and Hannah sat on a couch in his parents' family room, with Olivia between them and his parents sitting on the adjacent love seat. While Hannah held Olivia's hand, Mason worked to calm her fears and avoid a meltdown. For once, he actually sympathized with his parents. They'd been desperate when he'd arrived, not sure how to help Olivia. Her usual shadow, Wyatt, was in a meeting not answering their calls or texts, and they were at their wit's end.

It took nearly an hour to explain everything, answer her questions and get her back to her usual, bubbly self. Like a switch being flipped, it was as if none of the earlier hysterics had ever happened.

"How long will you be here?" she asked, as if he was on vacation and they hadn't just gone around and around about Audrey's murder.

He was saved from answering when Wyatt walked in. He stopped, his jaw tightening when he saw them.

Olivia's face lit up with happiness. "Wyatt. Look. Mason finally came to visit."

"I see that. Mason, Hannah." He gave his parents a

hard look as he crossed to Olivia and kissed her fore-head. "Everything okay, sweetie?"

"Everything's perfect. It's so good to see Mason again. Isn't it?"

"Of course. It's time for your meds. I got you a refill on my way over."

"Oh, thanks, Wyatt." She stood and took the little pillbox he handed her, then headed into the kitchen.

He crossed to the love seat and kissed his mother's forehead. "Mom, good to see you. Dad."

She smiled just as brightly as Olivia had. "Sorry to disturb your busy schedule with all those messages. I didn't know what else to do."

"It's no problem. I came as soon as I could." He sat in the recliner that faced the couch and eyed Mason with a lack of enthusiasm. "I heard some of what you were telling Olivia as I was parking my gun in the foyer. The charges against you have been dropped?"

He nodded, not particularly interested in striking up a conversation with his brother.

"I guess you'll be leaving soon, then. Heading back to Tennessee."

"We've got a few more loose ends to tie up."

"Like what?"

"Like finding out who set me up for Audrey's forced suicide."

Wyatt stared at him. "Forced suicide? What does that even mean?"

"I thought you heard everything in the foyer. The ME said she actually shot herself, and then someone tried to frame me after the fact. That same person is likely the one who somehow coerced her to shoot herself and then wiped the gun clean and left it for me to pick up. The FBI's looking into all of it as part of the conspiracy charges, so hopefully it will be figured out soon. There's some DNA evidence that proves someone else was there. Just a matter of time before we get a profile. Then, it's a matter of getting a warrant for a DNA sample from all of Audrey's known contacts. Shouldn't be too hard. The PI we hired already provided a list to the Chief." He frowned. "Come to think of it. Your name was on that list. I didn't realize you and Audrey were an item."

Mason caught Hannah's surprised look, but she quickly masked it, nodding as if in agreement with his bogus claim about the DNA. Wyatt, on the other hand, wasn't masking his surprise well at all. The fact that he'd gone pale had Mason all the more determined to keep his team digging into his past. Something wasn't right here. And although he'd never peg his brother as a killer, he'd bet his entire fortune that Wyatt knew something and for some reason was hiding it.

"Your source is misinformed," Wyatt said, his usual indifference back in place. "I've seen her around town a few times, but we certainly weren't an item."

Mason shrugged. "That's for the FBI to decide I suppose. Doesn't matter anyway. Obviously your DNA wouldn't be a match."

"Obviously not."

Hannah blinked innocently. "Wasn't there some DNA evidence in Landon's case the police are looking at too?"

Mason grinned. She was playing Watson to his Sherlock.

"Landon?" Wyatt swore, then glanced at their mother. "Sorry." He looked at Mason again. "Are you digging up ancient history? Dragging our family through that awfulness again?"

"When I saw you at the hospital, I thought you said the family was still concerned about what had happened to Landon? Don't you want to know who killed Mandy and framed him?"

His father's face scrunched in anger. "Mason, don't you dare go stirring up trouble again."

"Mr. Ford, are you kidding—"

Mason put his hand on Hannah's arm to stop her.

She clamped her mouth shut.

He winked, and she relaxed against him, letting out a deep breath.

"What DNA?" Wyatt asked. "Hannah said there was something in Landon's case."

"Now, son—"

"Dad, I want to hear this." Wyatt motioned to him and their father fell silent. "Go on, Mason. What all-important piece of evidence have you dug up that's worth making our lives miserable again? And jeopardizing my business? I could lose clients."

"Just some testing being performed on the clothes that were cut off Mandy DuBois in the hospital. We should have results anytime now. They're testing every drop of blood, looking for DNA from whoever fired the gun that killed her. Just like with the DNA in Audrey's case, they feel they'll be able to wrap everything up really soon."

Hannah nodded. "Yep. It's all coming together. Isn't that wonderful?"

"Thrilling," Wyatt said, his eyes flashing with annoyance.

Olivia stepped into the room from the kitchen, her hands tight around a glass of ice water. "Wyatt? What's he talking about? Mason, you didn't say anything to me about DNA."

Wyatt stood and crossed to her. "Don't get worked up. It's standard police stuff."

Mason gave her a reassuring smile. "I didn't mean to worry you. We think we'll be able to point to Mandy's real killer is all. And figure out who tried to frame me in Audrey's case. After that, we'll never have to worry about these cases again."

Wyatt put his arm around her and narrowed his eyes at Mason.

Hannah nudged him. "I'm expecting that package at my house. I have to be there to sign for it, remember?"

"Oh yeah. Right. We need to go." They both stood. "Mom, Dad, we'll see ourselves out. Take care, Olivia." He and Hannah headed out of the room and into the long foyer. He couldn't wait to get out of the house and away from the people he called family.

He'd just reached for the doorknob when Hannah stopped him.

"Wait, your gun." She opened the box on top of a decorative table against the wall. His and Wyatt's guns were both there. She started to pick one up, then hesitated, her eyes widening. She gave him a sharp look before setting it down and taking the other one instead.

"Is there a problem?" Wyatt stood at the other end of the foyer, looking at them.

"Uh, no, of course not." She seemed shaken as she handed Mason his gun.

He gave her a questioning look but she shook her head, so he didn't say anything.

"Another great visit with you, Wyatt." Mason pulled open the door. "Let's do it again real soon." He ushered Hannah outside.

Chapter Twenty

As soon as they were out of sight of the Ford home, Hannah let out a pent-up breath. "That was fun."

He grinned. "It was once you started playing detective with me. I think we really rattled Wyatt."

"You think he killed Mandy? And threatened or confused Audrey into shooting herself?"

"I guess it's possible, especially if Audrey was heavily medicated. But I'm more inclined to think since the mayor was the one heading up the conspiracy to frame Landon, and Wyatt's obviously financially involved in the dealings the mayor had, that he knows something about why Mandy was killed and who killed her. And why Landon was framed. The bastard's more worried about escaping justice for his own crimes than catching whoever is indirectly responsible for Landon being murdered in prison."

"I think there's far more to it than that." She looked out the window. "I know we were bluffing, saying we had to go to my house. But since we're about to pass the turnoff and it's closer than the estate, let's swing in there. I need to show you something."

Without a word, he turned down the next road, then moments later headed up the long unpaved driveway that led to her home. He winced as the rental car hit a pothole. "I can see why you have an SUV. Ever think about having this thing paved?"

"It would ruin the old-world charm."

He smiled and pulled to a stop in front of her house. "I don't like you living out this far from other homes. Doesn't feel safe."

"I've been here for years, never an incident. Come on. This is important."

When they were inside, she pulled him to the couch and tugged him down beside her.

His brows shot up in surprise. "You really are in a hurry. What's so important?"

"Take out your gun."

"What?"

"Take out your gun."

"O...kay. It's loaded. Be careful."

She shook her head. "I don't want it. I want you to turn it over, look at the bottom."

Frowning, he turned it over, careful to keep the muzzle pointed away from her. "Ah, hell. I've got Wyatt's gun. I'll have to see him once more before I leave to give it back to him."

"Mason. That's not Wyatt's gun."

"Well of course it is. There are three grooves on the bottom. Mine only has two."

"Look closer."

He held it up to the light, tilting the gun back and forth. He suddenly stiffened.

She nodded as if he'd spoken. "I saw it too, in your parents' foyer. I took his on purpose to show you. The first groove is just like the one you showed me on your gun earlier today. The other two are different. Close, but different. Definitely not done by the same tool."

He slowly shook his head. "It's Landon's gun. Wyatt must have made more grooves to make it seem like his own gun. Which means the gun at Landon's trial was actually Wyatt's. No one ever thought to look at the grooves on the bottom to be sure. We all assumed it was Landon's. Just that someone else had faked the evidence to make it seem that Landon's gun was the one that killed Mandy. My God, Hannah. Wyatt must have killed Mandy, and framed Landon."

"I knew I should have gotten rid of the dang thing years ago."

Mason and Hannah jerked around to see Wyatt standing in the opening to her hallway. He aimed an identical-looking gun, Mason's gun, at Mason's head. "Drop it or I shoot your girlfriend."

Mason pitched his dead brother's gun onto the floor. "How'd you get here ahead of us?"

"A little shortcut I know about. It's hell on a car's undercarriage, but I knew my only chance to get the drop on you was the element of surprise."

"Why did you keep Landon's gun? So no one would be suspicious when you no longer had it? Considering your own gun was locked up in evidence?"

"You always were too smart for your own good. I had to carve those grooves on the bottom so no one would ask why I no longer had my gun. But all the while I prayed no one would think to check for grooves on the one at the trial. Honestly, I was stunned that no one did. I was on pins and needles for months expecting that to happen. All these years, no one noticed the difference in the grooves I'd made. Until Hannah did back at Dad's house. I knew she was acting funny as she picked up your gun. Of course, after you left and I looked at mine, I knew she must have figured it out and would tell you. I thought you'd run to the FBI or police as soon as you signed for the package you mentioned. Luckily, you didn't."

Mason shifted on the couch as Wyatt moved into the room, obviously trying to shield Hannah.

She cursed herself for being in such a hurry to come inside that she didn't even bring her purse from the car. If she had, she might have been able to get her own gun and surprise Wyatt.

"What did you do?" Mason asked him, probably stalling for time as they both tried to figure a way out of this that didn't end with either or both of them dead. "After you killed Mandy, you realized you'd have to leave your gun there since ballistics would match it, and take Landon's?"

"You think you have it all figured out, don't you?"

"I'm getting there. Unfortunately, not soon enough to save Mandy and Audrey. Or Landon."

His eyes flashed with anger. "Audrey killed herself. You told us that tonight. It was a suicide."

"Not if someone else was there, and they coerced her. Someone had to wipe the gun clean and put it upstairs after she shot herself."

"Well it sure wasn't me."

"What about Mandy? There's no other explanation for you having Landon's gun. You shot her, then framed your own brother and let him go to prison for it. You might as well be the one who killed him in prison. If it wasn't for you, he wouldn't have been there."

"Not true. I didn't kill Mandy. I haven't killed anyone."

"If that's the case, why are you pointing a gun at us?"

His jaw tightened. "Because I need you to listen. All this digging and DNA crap you're so proud of, all it's going to do is destroy what's left of our family. You need to stop and fix it, before it's too late."

Mason subtly shifted again, and Hannah realized he was trying to position himself closer to her end table. A heavy paperweight in the shape of a small ball was sitting there. Was he hoping to throw it at Wyatt?

"It's the DNA that's got you scared, isn't it? When I mentioned testing all the blood on Mandy's shirt, you went pale."

"For good reason. Just whose DNA do you think you'll find if you complete those tests?"

"Yours. Obviously."

"Wrong." Wyatt's hand tightened on the gun as he stepped closer. "Olivia's."

Mason had been slowly moving his hand toward the side table, but Wyatt's statement stopped him cold. "What the hell are you talking about?"

"The truth. Olivia's blood is on Mandy's shirt. If you don't stop this train you've got going down the tracks, it's going to run over her and destroy her."

"Put the gun down. I'm not calling the police. Put it down and tell me what you're talking about."

"No way. I don't trust you. But I will tell you what happened. Because you're forcing my hand. If you'd left it alone, she wouldn't be in danger. All these years I've done nothing but try to protect Olivia. And you came down here and destroyed my efforts in a matter of days."

"Wyatt—"

"Olivia killed Mandy. Her blood is on the shirt because they fought. They were tangled up with each other when Mandy got a good punch in and bloodied Olivia's nose. It bled all over her shirt. Mandy was so angry she pulled Landon's gun out of the side table. Olivia was forced to shoot her, in self-defense. But she panicked, and ran."

"There are all kinds of gaps in that story. You're covering for yourself."

Hannah pressed a hand to her chest. She couldn't believe what she was hearing. And from the disbelief and horror in Mason's voice, he couldn't either.

"No. I'm not. Since Olivia wasn't old enough for dad to have given her a gun yet, she stole mine and used it to threaten Mandy. She didn't mean to hurt her, but she did. After she shot her, she dropped the gun, then panicked and grabbed it again and ran. Except she grabbed Landon's by mistake and left mine. And by running, she left Landon to find Mandy and you know the rest. That's why she's been so torn up all these years. She can't handle the guilt of what she did, that Landon went to prison and died for her crime. I swear to you, Mason. If I could have saved Landon, I would have."

"I'm not buying any of this," Mason said. "I know you were involved in the corruption, that you and the mayor were laundering money. And someone faked GSR results against Landon. And misplaced evidence that would have exonerated him. Olivia couldn't have done that."

Wyatt swore. "You really have been digging. As for my activities, sure, I laundered some money for him. There's your confession. Too bad the statute of limitations has expired on those crimes. Trust me. I checked. After Olivia killed Mandy and I realized it was my gun she'd used, it shook me to the core. I cleaned up my act and dedicated myself to helping her."

"Is he right?" Hannah asked. "About the statute of limitations."

Mason nodded. "He did his homework. But there's no statute of limitations on murder."

Wyatt's throat worked. "Which is why I'm trying to talk some sense into you. You and that fancy company of yours and all these people you brought to town to work on your investigations, you need to put the brakes on. Somehow. Or you're going to send Olivia to prison."

"Make me believe you, Wyatt. Make me believe your story. Then we can discuss Olivia. But first, put the gun away."

"So you can attack me? Or shoot me? No thanks. I know all about that famous sense of justice you have. You still think I'm the bad guy in this. Until you believe otherwise, you're going to try to take me out."

Mason swore. "Then at least turn the muzzle away from my head."

Wyatt relented, and turned it, but only a little. In a heartbeat he could point it right back at him.

"Go on. Convince me that our fifteen-year-old sister at the time is a murderer. And then explain how you're not the one who framed Landon for the murder. Because there's no way Olivia did."

"I'm not saying she's a murderer. It was an accident."

Mason waited, without saying anything else.

Wyatt glanced at Hannah as if hoping she could help him make Mason see reason. "You made Olivia quit her job working for the mayor to protect her. Well it was too late. She was already having an affair with him."

Hannah gasped in shock.

"You're lying," Mason gritted out.

"I'm not. I'm telling you the truth. Mandy found out. I don't know how, but she did, and she called Olivia and told her she was going to tell the police and they'd arrest him for statutory rape. Olivia fancied herself in love with the mayor and didn't want anything to happen to him. She stole my gun and confronted Mandy. After she shot her, by accident, she ran out. She made the anonymous 911 call to try to save Mandy. It didn't occur to her that Landon might end up taking the blame. She ran to the mayor, told him what had happened. Naturally, he wanted to protect his secrets from coming out, so he told her not to tell anyone. Later, once Landon was charged, he convinced her to keep quiet, saying he'd make sure he got off. But of course we all know how that turned out."

He held his free hand out in supplication. "Why do you think Olivia had so many issues after Landon's death? It was guilt. All this time, she's been struggling with that guilt. It's a terrible burden."

"Drop the gun, Wyatt." Olivia's voice rang out.

He jerked toward her, then turned the gun away. She was standing in the hallway where he'd emerged just minutes earlier, holding her own gun. "What are you doing, Olivia? Put that away."

"No." Her hands shook as she held both of them around the pistol. "I knew you were up to something when you drove off right after they left." A single tear slid down her cheek. "I won't let you kill Mason."

"Kill Mason? Sweetie, I'm not going to shoot him. I just wanted him to listen to me telling him…"

"What?" Another tear slid down her face. "Telling him how awful I am? That I'm the reason Landon died?" She sobbed, the gun dipping.

Mason stood.

Wyatt whirled around, pointing his gun at him. "Stay there."

"No." Olivia sniffed and steadied her gun at Wyatt again. "I don't want him hurt. I didn't save Landon. But I can save Mason." The gun was shaking so much that Hannah was surprised it didn't go off.

"What about me?" Wyatt asked. "I've helped you all these years. And now Mason's trying to frame me, say I had something to do with Audrey's death. Does that seem fair, Olivia?"

Her lower lip trembled. "No," she whispered. "It's not fair."

A look of relief crossed his face. "He's trying to hurt you, and me. Shoot him, Olivia."

She swung her gun toward Mason.

Hannah slid to the floor at his feet, her hand covering her mouth.

"Whoa, whoa," Mason cajoled, holding his hands out placatingly toward Olivia. "Both of you put your guns down and let's figure this out."

"Go on," Wyatt urged. "Shoot him. All your pain, everything that's happening, is his fault."

"Mason's fault?" Her lower lip wobbled, as if she was fighting the urge to cry.

"That's right," Wyatt said. "It's Mason's fault."

"Don't listen to him, Olivia. He's trying to blame you for Mandy's murder. He said you shot her."

Her face crumpled. "Because I did."

Mason slowly shook his head. "No. You didn't."

"I did. She was going to tell on me. We fought. I got scared and I—"

"You pointed a gun at her. But you didn't fire it."

A look of confusion crossed her face. "I didn't?"

"He's lying to you," Wyatt called out.

Hannah didn't have a clue what Mason was trying, but he shifted on his feet, and the toe of his right shoe nudged Landon's gun out from under the coffee table where it must have landed. Another subtle shift and he nudged it again. She realized he was very much aware that she was on the floor, and knew that might give them a chance. Carefully, ever so slowly, she inched her fingers toward the gun that Wyatt had altered.

"I'm not lying." Mason's voice was calm, like when he'd talked her down at his parents' house earlier. "And

I can prove it. Where were you standing when Mandy was shot?"

Her brow wrinkled. "Right beside her. We were arguing. She hit my nose. The gun went off." She shuddered.

"And was Mandy holding a gun?"

She shook her head. "No."

"Olivia, you don't know what you're saying," Wyatt said. "She had Landon's gun. Remember?"

"No, I...she didn't have a gun. I had Landon's gun. I took it from the side table where he normally keeps it."

"Olivia—"

"Shut up, Wyatt. I'm trying to think."

His face reddened.

Hannah stretched her hand a little more. She couldn't screw this up. She couldn't let Wyatt see her moving toward the gun on the floor.

"Olivia." Mason's voice was soft, gentle. "The gun the police ran ballistics on, the gun that killed Mandy, was Wyatt's gun."

She shook her head. "No. I had Landon's gun."

"That's right. But the person who killed Mandy was standing in the kitchen opening. I had a crime scene reconstructions specialist prove that. She wasn't shot at close range. Wyatt was standing in the kitchen. He must have found out you were going there and followed you. I'm not sure. Only he knows that. But Wyatt's gun is the one with the three grooves on the bottom that dad carved, and that's the gun left at the scene that night. It was the gun that fired the fatal shot. You grabbed Landon's gun, thinking it was Wyatt's. He let Landon take the blame, and then made you think all these years that you'd shot her, when he's the one who shot her."

She was shaking her head back and forth. "No, no, no. You said you would prove it."

"I can. We'll get the gun from evidence and see it has three lines on the bottom, lines that Dad made. It's Wyatt's gun in evidence. When we were at the house earlier tonight, Hannah saw the gun Wyatt had in the basket, on the foyer table. And she saw that two of the grooves weren't like the others. That's because Wyatt carved those grooves himself. Hannah took his gun to show me, and left mine. Wyatt's holding my gun. And his gun, the one he's carried for the last eight years, is under the coffee table. It's Landon's gun, the one that Wyatt used to kill Mandy. And the only way he can have Landon's gun is if his gun is the one they thought was Landon's at the trial."

He looked at Wyatt, his face mirroring his disgust. "You let a fifteen-year-old think she'd killed someone when you're the one who did it, likely to protect your money laundering scheme. You knew the mayor was molesting her and didn't want Mandy to report him and ruin your little venture together. When you somehow realized that Olivia was going to confront Mandy, you followed her, and decided to take advantage of the situation. You were able to keep Olivia silent about the mayor by feeding her guilt about the crime. And you let Landon take the fall. Good grief, did none of that ever bother you?"

His face scrunched up with anger. "Landon. Knew."

Hannah and Mason both froze and stared at him.

"It's true," Olivia whispered. "I told him, in jail, what I'd done. I said I'd confess and get him out, but…" She blinked, and a look of dawning crossed her face. "But Wyatt convinced both of us it would work out. The evidence would prove Landon didn't do it. If I just stayed quiet, he'd get off and I wouldn't get into trouble." She lifted the gun ever so slightly, aiming it at Wyatt's head. "You killed her and let me think I'd killed her. And then you let Landon die."

He whipped his pistol around to point at her, his face contorted in rage. "I could have killed both of you that day, you and Mandy, to keep the mayor's secret. But I didn't. I protected you, and kept protecting you, all these years."

"You used me," she yelled. "To cover your crimes. And you let Landon die."

"No. You did. Just who do you think killed him in prison? Your lover, that's who. The mayor was worried that Landon's appeals against his conviction would reveal the truth about his relationship with you. Landon's death is your fault. Not mine."

She let out a keening moan. But she kept the gun trained on him.

"Stop it, Wyatt," Mason ordered, his face red with anger. "How dare you try to pin any of this on Olivia. She was a kid, fifteen. The mayor wasn't her lover. He was her rapist. If the truth had come out, he'd have been convicted of statutory rape and you would have gone to prison for the illegal schemes and money laundering you both did together."

Olivia's eyes widened. "Money laundering? I don't understand. Wyatt? What did you do?"

Wyatt swore and narrowed his eyes at her.

Hannah was finally able to grab Landon's gun. But she didn't raise it. Her angle was all wrong. The only person she could clearly hit from where she sat was Olivia. Not Wyatt. She kept it down on the floor and pressed it against Mason's leg. He shifted again and slowly sat down.

Wyatt glanced at him. "Don't move."

"Just sitting."

Wyatt frowned.

"Drop your gun, Wyatt," Olivia ordered again. "You have to pay for your sins. Mason's going to arrest you."

"Arrest me?" He laughed. "He's not even a cop anymore."

She frowned.

Wyatt centered his gun on Olivia's chest. "You made me do this."

Bam! Bam!

Olivia's eyes widened in shock. The gun dropped from her fingertips as she stared at Wyatt.

Wyatt frowned in confusion as he watched her, obviously looking for blood. But there wasn't any. He blinked, then blinked again. He staggered forward, then looked down at his chest where a red wet stain was slowly spreading across his shirt. He turned his head toward Mason, and only then noticed Landon's still-smoking pistol in his hand. The gun he'd scooped up just as Wyatt was about to shoot Olivia.

Wyatt slowly crumpled to the floor.

Chapter Twenty-One

Hannah clasped her arms around her waist as she sat on her front porch steps beside Mason nearly two weeks later. It was the only way she could keep herself from reaching for him. After all, it would only cause her more heartbreak. Because there was no way he was staying here now, not after Wyatt's death and he'd had Olivia temporarily committed to a mental hospital. And there was certainly no way *she* was leaving *her* family. They were two people who deeply cared about each other, but could never be together. Sometimes life really sucked.

His rental car was a few yards away, packed and ready. He'd stopped to give her an update on the case and to say goodbye on his way to the airport.

"How's Olivia holding up?" she asked.

"She's having a tough time. It'll take a while to beat the addiction to the drugs Wyatt was feeding her." He shook his head. "I still can't believe none of us realized he was doping her all this time, rehashing his mythical version of Mandy's murder, reinforcing her guilt so she wouldn't think about what really happened that night and out him as the killer. If she hadn't gone into withdrawal after Wyatt's death when her pills ran out, we might never have known she was addicted to drugs. We might never have figured out the truth."

"Well you're helping her now. Fighting your parents in court yesterday to get guardianship over her so she could get the treatment she needs had to be incredibly hard. But now Olivia will have a chance at a real future. You really are her hero. You're giving her back her life."

"Tell that to my parents. As far as they're concerned, the hearing was one more nail in my coffin. Especially after Wyatt's death."

"They should be thanking you for saving their daughter instead of blaming you."

He pressed his cheek against the top of her head. "You're a good friend, Hannah Cantrell."

The word *friend* had her wincing. Luckily, he couldn't see her face right now.

"I got a call from Knoll a little while ago."

"Uh-oh. Why would the district attorney call you?"

"Don't sound so worried. It was about the DNA testing. My bluff about them finding DNA in Audrey's case turned out to be fact. They found touch DNA on Audrey's forehead. It matched Wyatt."

"Wait. Are you saying he's the one who was at her house when she was shot? He kissed her, then what? Convinced her to kill herself?"

"We may never know the full truth. But he was lying about the money laundering being in the past. He was still into all kinds of illegal activities around here. But he left enough in his journals at home to tie a lot of the loose ends together. I got to read some of the more enlightening entries. Like that he'd found out about my crime scene expert and the theory about a shooter being in Mandy's kitchen. He knew I would never stop. So he decided to use Audrey as his pawn, knowing how vulnerable she was at the end, with her illness. He's the one who put her up to the Gatlinburg visit, the abduction. He'd planned on framing me for her murder. It was all part of his plan to stop me once and for all. If he'd just killed me, shot me from a distance, he'd probably have gotten away with everything. But he wanted me to suffer. He wanted me humiliated. He'd planned to have me killed while in jail. If you hadn't helped me escape at the station, I'd definitely be dead right now. Thank you."

"You're very welcome. Did his journal say anything about how Audrey died? How he got her to do it?"

"Unfortunately, no. But the ME said she had high levels of painkillers in her system. Much higher than the recommended dose. It's likely that Wyatt had something to do with that, then somehow tricked her to pull the trigger."

"How sad."

"Very. She didn't deserve that." He was silent for a few minutes. "Something else Knoll told me. He got the final DNA comparisons back on Mandy DuBois's clothing from the lab I hired. It corroborated the story Olivia and Wyatt told. It was Olivia's blood, likely from the nosebleed Mandy caused when she punched her."

"It's a shame the clothes weren't tested when Landon was arrested."

"Actually, given the conspiracy in place, the results

would have likely disappeared and wouldn't have made a difference in his trial. But at least having them now helps paint the full picture of what actually happened. Knoll said her family is deeply appreciative that we figured out who the killer was. They never believed Landon did it. Now they have some closure."

"Everywhere you go, people are better because of it."

He looked down at her. "I can name dozens of people who wouldn't agree with that sentiment."

"I can name dozens who would. And *my* dozens aren't families of criminals involved in corruption."

He laughed, then gently disentangled his arm from hers. "I'd better go. My team's probably at the airport getting antsy to get home to their loved ones. Private plane or not, they have a schedule to keep."

He jogged down the steps, then turned to look up at her. He opened his mouth several times to say something else, then seemed to think better of it. He finally just smiled and walked away. He'd left her, again. And this time, he wasn't coming back.

Chapter Twenty-Two

Mason pitched his phone onto his kitchen counter. Calling his parents had been a mistake, one he'd never make again. Even a month after Wyatt's death, they weren't willing to forgive him. The fact that Wyatt had hurt their daughter and caused the death of their oldest son, and that Mason had shot Wyatt to save Olivia's life, didn't seem to matter. There was too much water under the bridge. And there was no forgiveness in their hearts for their one remaining son. They continued to blame him for every bad thing that had happened.

He picked up the shot glass full of whiskey he'd just poured. It would be his first since leaving Beauchamp. But he sincerely doubted it would be his last. After all, he had an anniversary to mourn. It had been exactly one month since he lost the woman he'd realized far too late meant more to him than drawing his next breath.

He tossed the shot back, then crossed to the glass doors that opened onto his backyard. Only it wasn't really *his* yard today. It belonged to his team. As he did every holiday, he celebrated with them and their families one day early so he didn't interfere with their private gatherings. Thanksgiving was no different.

There were all kinds of games set up outside, from archery to cornhole, to a rowdy game of poker on the back deck. But with the sun going down, everyone was settling into chairs that had been arranged in a huge circle around the roaring firepit—much like the firepit back in Beauchamp. Only instead of talking about a murder investigation, they'd carry on the tradition of talking about what each of them was thankful for this year.

"You gonna stay in here the rest of the day and get drunk?"

Mason turned to see Bryson leaning against the kitchen island, arms crossed.

"Sounds like a good idea."

"It sounded like a good idea to me too, after being shot and relegated to a wheelchair. I'd probably still be in that chair if you hadn't refused to let me give up. You gave me hope again, the will to rejoin the world rather than spend the rest of my days sick and alone and feeling sorry for myself."

Mason turned back to the glass doors. "Our situations are different. Besides, Teagan is the one who gave you hope. I can't take that credit."

Bryson stopped beside him. "You're the reason I met Teagan, so it's basically the same. And your situation doesn't seem all that different to me. I'd given up. You've given up." He reached past Mason and slid open one of the glass doors, then paused. "I don't know whether or not you realize it, but Hannah looks at you the same way Teagan looks at me. Like she's discovered the missing half of her soul. That's rare, a precious gift to be treasured and cherished, not tossed aside when things get complicated. It all boils down to one question. Is she worth fighting for? If the answer is yes, then what the hell are you still doing here?" He left Mason standing there and joined the others around the fire pit.

Mason stared out the back door, Bryson's parting words replaying through his mind.

Is she worth fighting for?

He closed his eyes, remembering.

Hannah, sitting at her father's desk when Mason locked himself in the office at the police station while trying to escape. She was beautiful and poised, charming him with her saucy *Well, this is awkward* comment. Then later, surprising him when he found out she'd been pointing a gun at him beneath the desk. She was so brave, smart, unexpected. And such a warrior, never relenting in her fight to prove his innocence. Willing to sacrifice her own future to fight for what she felt was right.

Another memory. Hannah, throwing her expensive phone out the window without hesitation to keep the police from tracking their location.

Hannah, mowing down small trees and practically destroying her SUV without thinking twice about it just because she wanted to protect him.

Hannah, at the cottage, tears streaming down her face, telling him she was already half in love with him, and afraid that she wouldn't survive if she fell the rest of the way and he left her.

He braced himself against the doorframe, looking past the tables overflowing with food, the bows and arrows scattered in the grass, beanbags lying on the cornhole board—the trappings of people who cared deeply about one another, a family by choice if not by blood. He treasured each and every one of them. And yet he felt empty inside.

Is she worth fighting for?

He swore and grabbed a set of keys from a peg beside the door. Then he headed outside. When he reached the circle around the firepit, instead of taking the last remaining seat, he stopped in front of Bryson's chair. Everyone fell silent. Mason tossed the ring of keys to Bryson.

"What are these?"

"House keys. I need you to lock up after everyone leaves."

Bryson arched a brow. "Any particular reason?"

"You asked me a question earlier. The answer is *yes*, she's worth it." Mason glanced around the circle. "Happy Thanksgiving, everyone. If you'll excuse me, I have a plane to catch. Looks like I might be eating mudbugs for Thanksgiving."

The team cheered as he jogged toward the house.

Chapter Twenty-Three

"You're his *family*," Hannah snarled into the phone to Mason's father as she paced in the side yard past her parents' garage. "It's Thanksgiving, for crying out loud. Did it even occur to you to invite Mason? Does it bother you to think about your son in Gatlinburg, without any family, while you stuff your faces on food his money probably bought? You've banished him from your lives. Why? Because you care about what some silly neighbors think? Or that the family of one of the corrupt jerks he helped put in prison throws a few rolls of toilet paper on your house? Seriously? Do you realize how petty that sounds?"

"Now look here, young lady," he said.

"No, Mr. Ford. You look here. Mason is one of the most honest, decent men I've ever known. He has more integrity in one pinkie than your whole family combined. I asked you to call him, to try to repair some of the damage you've done over the years. To let the one son that you have left know he's worthy of your love, and that you're sorry. But you know what? Forget it. You don't deserve the wonderful son God gifted you with.

Because you're too selfish and blind to even know what you threw away. Well, I'm not. I know what I lost. I just pray it's not too late to tell him I love him. He deserves to know there's at least one person in this world who truly, deeply cares about him."

She ended the call and shoved her phone in her pocket. When she turned around to go back inside, she froze in shock. A very tall, extremely handsome man in a navy blue suit stood just a few feet away, his warm brown eyes locked on her.

"M-Mason?"

"Hello, Hannah. Were you talking to my family?"

Her face flushed hot with mortification. "Your father, actually. I'm so sorry. I swear I didn't plan on berating him or your family. But when I asked him to wish you a Happy Thanksgiving, and found out they weren't even talking to you anymore, I just lost it. I couldn't—"

"Don't apologize." He stepped close, making her belly do crazy things as she stared up at him. "I've made excuses for my family for so long that I couldn't even see them for who they really are. But my eyes are wide open now. Thanks to you. I'm moving on."

"Moving on?" Afraid to hope, she simply waited.

He threaded his fingers through hers. "I owe you an apology. You offered me your love, and I couldn't see past my bitterness and hatred of this place to accept that miraculous gift. It didn't take me long to realize the mistake I'd made. But it took me far too long to try to make things right."

"Mason, I—"

He pulled a phone out of his pocket. "I meant to give you this before I left and forgot."

She took the phone, her stomach dropping in disappointment. "You came here, on Thanksgiving Day, to replace my phone?"

"Well, that wasn't the only reason."

Hope flared inside her. But instead of kissing her or professing his love like she desperately wanted, he tugged her past the end of the garage, then motioned toward the driveway. Confused, she looked at the collection of cars belonging to her parents and sisters. But there was another car now. A shiny new blue Tucson with a big red bow on top.

She pressed her hand to her chest. "You didn't!"

"I did." He handed her a metal key ring with a fob attached. "It has all the goodies, just like you asked."

She shook her head, frantically holding the key fob out to him. "Mason, no. I was joking when I said you could buy me a new car. I never wanted your money."

He ignored the key. "Well you'll have to take my money anyway. It comes with me. Because I want you. Yesterday. Today. Tomorrow. In my life, with me. Always." He pressed a tender kiss against her lips. "I'm not asking you to marry me. Not yet. I'm thinking I'll take you on a few dates first." He winked, which had her whole body flushing with heat.

"I'm going to court you, Hannah Cantrell. I'm going to turn on the charm and wear you down until you can't live without me. Then I'll get on bended knee and pop the question. Consider yourself forewarned."

"Mason—"

"I was a fool to expect you to give up your family, your home. I realize that now. We can live here, in Beauchamp. I could buy the Fontenot estate, if you want. Or a town house in the historic district. Or we can build something brand-new. All that matters is that we're together."

"You…you would do that? Move here, to a place you hate? Just so you can be with me?"

"If that's what it takes to make you mine, I'll do that, and more. I'm in love with you, have been probably from the moment you pointed Wesley at me in your father's office. But until you taught me what real love was, I didn't recognize it. Now I do. Whatever you want, name it. If it's within my power, I'll make it yours. All I ask in return is that you give me a chance to show you that we really can have a future together."

She burst into tears.

His face fell. "Hannah?"

"Happy tears," she gasped between sobs. "Really happy tears."

His expression turned hopeful. "Then I'm not totally crazy here? To think we can make this work?"

She wiped her eyes, smearing makeup on her fingers. "After everything you've been through in this town, you're willing to stay here, for me…" She struggled for words. "You don't need to move back here, Mason. I'm willing to move to Gatlinburg."

He frowned. "That's not fair to you. What about your family?"

"Sarah and Mary have their own families in other towns. And my parents, as soon as Dad's fully recovered, are going on a whirlwind RV tour to work on their bucket list. There's nothing here for me anymore. But even if there was, I'd still be willing to move somewhere else. You aren't the only one who realized what a mistake they'd made over the past month. Being without you has been agony. I don't want to let one more day pass without you in my life. And you sure don't have to court me, although I think the idea is exquisitely romantic. I'm ready for that question, Mason. Ask me."

"I don't have a ring."

She tossed the metal key ring with the fob to him. "Yes. You do."

He threw his head back, laughing with such a joyful sound it brought more tears to her eyes. Still chuckling, he dropped to one knee on the driveway and held the key ring up in the air. "Hannah Cantrell. Will you please do me the honor of being my wife?"

"Yes! Yes! Yes!" She held out her left hand, grinning as he slid the key ring onto her finger.

He swooped her up against his chest and spun around in a circle, both of them laughing.

The sound of a door banging open and excited shrieking was their only warning before they were surrounded by the entire Landry clan, including two toddlers and a pair of barking retrievers.

Mason carefully set Hannah on her feet. The look of bewilderment and wariness on his face as he eyed her clapping, laughing, smiling parents, sisters, brothers-in-law, niece and nephew nearly broke her heart. He'd been treated so badly by his own family that he didn't seem to recognize the love and acceptance on each and every one of her family members' faces.

Her father, leaning on a cane, held out his hand. "Welcome to the family, son."

Mason's eyes widened. His Adam's apple bobbed in his throat before he took the offered hand and shook it. "Thank you, sir."

"Call me Dad," her father corrected.

He stared at him a long moment, as if struggling to speak. "Dad." His voice was raw and gritty.

Her mother shoved between them and slid her arms around Mason's waist. He hesitated, obviously not sure what to do.

"Hug me, son," her mother ordered. "The Landrys are huggers. And you're one of us now. You'll have to learn to hug every time we come to visit or go home. Heck, sometimes just because we enter a room."

He blinked several times, and Hannah realized he was fighting back tears. He put his arms around her mother, his breath coming out in a ragged exhale as he rested his cheek on the top of her head.

When he finally let go, her mother stepped back, her own eyes wet with tears. She cleared her throat, then motioned to the others. "Come on, everybody. The food's getting cold. Hannah, bring your young man inside, and let's get this holiday started."

"Yes, ma'am." Hannah held out her hand toward Mason as the rest of them hurried into the house. "Happy Thanksgiving, Mason."

He took her hand, his eyes full of wonder, no longer shadowed by the past. "Happy Thanksgiving, Hannah, my love. Now quit dawdling. Our family's waiting for us." He squeezed her hand and winked, his smile growing even brighter as they went into the house.

* * * * *

Look for more titles from Lena Diaz, coming soon!
And don't miss the previous books in
The Justice Seekers series:

Cowboy Under Fire
Agent Under Siege
Killer Conspiracy

Available now wherever
Harlequin Intrigue books are sold!

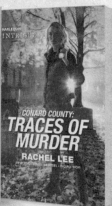

HARLEQUIN

*Uplifting or passionate,
heartfelt or thrilling—
Harlequin has your
happily-ever-after.*

With a wide range of romance series that each
offer new books every month, you are sure to
find the satisfying escape you deserve.

Look for all Harlequin series
new releases on the
last Tuesday of each month
in stores and online!

Harlequin.com

#2007 SAFEGUARDING THE SURROGATE
Mercy Ridge Lawmen • by Delores Fossen
Rancher Kara Holland's hot on the trail of a murderer who's been killing surrogates—like she was for her ill sister. But when Kara's trap goes terribly wrong, she's thrust headlong into the killer's crosshairs...along with her sister's widower, Deputy Daniel Logan.

#2008 THE TRAP
A Kyra and Jake Investigation • by Carol Ericson
When a new copycat killer strikes, Detective Jake McAllister and Kyra Chase race to find the mastermind behind LA's serial murders. Now, to protect the woman he loves, Jake must reveal a crucial secret about Kyra's past—the real reason The Player wants her dead.

#2009 PROFILING A KILLER
Behavioral Analysis Unit • by Nichole Severn
Special Agent Nicholas James knows serial killers. After all, he was practically raised by one and later became a Behavioral Analysis Unit specialist to enact justice. But Dr. Aubrey Flood's sister's murder is his highest-stakes case yet. Can Nicholas ensure Aubrey won't become the next victim?

#2010 UNCOVERING SMALL TOWN SECRETS
The Saving Kelby Creek Series • by Tyler Anne Snell
Detective Foster Lovett is determined to help his neighbor, Millie Dean, find her missing brother. But when Millie suddenly becomes a target, he finds himself facing the most dangerous case of his career...

#2011 K-9 HIDEOUT
A K-9 Alaska Novel • by Elizabeth Heiter
Police handler Tate Emory is thankful that Sabrina Jones saved his trusty K-9 companion, Sitka, but he didn't sign up for national media exposure. That exposure unveils his true identity to the dirty Boston cops he took down...and brings Sabrina's murderous stalker even closer to his target.

#2012 COLD CASE TRUE CRIME
An Unsolved Mystery Book • by Denise N. Wheatley
Samantha Vincent runs a true-crime blog, so when a friend asks her to investigate a murder, she's surprised to find the cops may want the case to go cold. Sam is confident she'll catch the killer when Detective Gregory Harris agrees to help her, but everything changes once she becomes a target...

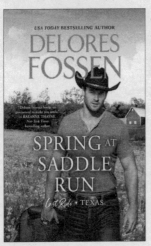